DAEMON'S BLADE

LOGAN BOOK ONE

DAEMON BLADE SERIES

LANA SKY

Daemon's Blade

Daemon's Blade By Lana Sky

———————)•••

Cover Design and Interior Formatting by Charity Chimni
Editing by Charity Chimni

Acknowledgments

Thanks so much to everyone who supported this draft along the way, including the many beta readers who provided encouragement! Please keep in mind that this story includes dark, graphic, and explicit content matter that may not be suitable for readers under the age of 18—or for readers who are uncomfortable with the following subject matter: mentions of abuse, explicit sex, and graphic depictions of violence.

PROLOGUE

After suffering in the bowels of a daemon prison for weeks, Logan Merris had become a connoisseur of torture smells. Singed hair. Dried blood. Puke. There was a predictable pattern to what one could expect when locked in a dark, dank room without light or hope.

Until now.

The new smell that tickled his nostrils was even worse than the rancid odor of decay.

"Hot dogs?" he grumbled, cringing at the concept of whatever mortals shoved into those meat sacks. So much for resisting his captors. He would crack in a heartbeat if they made him eat one of those things.

Not that he had much information to spill. Did they finally figure that out? He sure hoped not. Rumors ran rampant of what really happened in places like this when a prisoner couldn't afford bail. Organ harvesting. Slavery. Forced mercenary work.

All experiences he'd rather avoid. A smattering of advancing footsteps, however, merely compounded his unease.

He glanced at the cell door as two figures appeared through the iron bars. "This is him." The low voice drew his attention to one of the figures he recognized—the beefy bastard of a Raeth who had served as his lovely guard during his stay. The food scent emanated from him—apparently, hog dogs were the price he accepted to grant a visitor access to Haedyn's most vile prison.

At any rate, "tourist" was the best word to describe the slender woman lurking in his shadow. Unfortunately, her true identity was probably even worse. A lackey of a daemon lord? Or a more sinister foe—daemon hunters?

Her appearance didn't suggest either profession. Her body was sinfully shaped, and her skin pale enough to see bluish veins snaking beneath. Her hair was a bit too white for his tastes, and her eyes far too dark. The contrast made her seem ethereal against the backdrop of black stone surrounding her. Predictably, his cock lurched while his brain screamed a warning only one breed of women inspired. She was a daemon, and one he sensed wasn't to be trifled with, beautiful or not.

"Logan Merris, I think it's high time you earned your freedom," she said in a husky purr that was more sinister than sexy. Her English was crisp, and her accent was well defined —as if she knew which tongue he was more proficient in despite living in Hell. "It ought to be fairly easy for a man with your traits to accomplish what I want."

Logan spit out the blood still in his mouth from the last torture session. They'd whipped his back raw, and he could barely see straight from the resulting mixture of agony and arousal. Still, he attempted a smile. "What is that, sweetheart?"

The woman waved off her guard, who lumbered out of view. Then she inclined her head conspiratorially. He noted how the torchlight reflected off her eyes, but the effect didn't soften her expression. She looked dangerous, reminding him of a figure he didn't like to recall very often —his mother.

"Something any person with your track record wouldn't hesitate to do," she said, wrapping her manicured fingers around the bars of his cell. Her blood-red nails sparkled prettily in the firelight, reminding him just how much of the substance he'd lost to torture. He felt dizzy just sitting up straight.

"I want you to betray someone close to you for the greater good," she went on. "If it helps you sleep at night, think of it as saving the world. I'm sure you could use a good rest."

Logan winced. Was it a harmless taunt? Or did she perhaps know of the nightmare raging in his skull for the past year and a half...

One where the world was ablaze in fire, but he alone stood at the center of it all—the sole cause of the destruction.

Either way, he was getting damn tired of hearing about the apocalypse. Not too long ago, another figure had approached him with a similar offer, give or take. He considered telling this woman the same thing he'd said then.

To fuck off.

Considering that she stood on the other side of a jail cell, he was willing to entertain the subject a bit longer in this instance. Shifting on the pathetic lump of straw serving as his mattress, he sat forward and weighed his options. As it turned out, he didn't have many.

"What do I need to do?" he finally asked. No one could accuse him of sounding eager.

Not that the woman seemed to give a damn whether he was a willing accomplice or not. Her triumphant smirk was feral. "First, you'll answer the summons from your dear brother, Marcus."

Before he could question, she reached into the pocket of her skirt and withdrew a crisp slip of paper. While it resembled a plain piece of mortal letterhead, Logan wasn't fooled. It was a missive—an enchanted document intended to be read only by its target recipient. How this woman had managed to open one meant for him?

He didn't want to know.

"It appears he wants you to join him in the mortal realm," she said while scanning the page. "So much so that he even paid for your access to one of the official portal sites. Such the generous one, that Marcus."

Logan winced at the name. His first impulse was to deny he had a brother. Then he remembered...

He had two, after all—among many siblings he knew nothing about. A spotty family tree came with the territory when your mother was an evil bitch with a healthy libido.

Marcus, however, was a man he'd only met once—coincidentally, right before he wound up thrown in prison. Still, if the bastard had paid the hefty price to buy his passage through a portal…

He obviously wanted something.

"Why the hell should I care?" Logan asked out loud.

"Go to him," the woman continued, returning the slip to her pocket. "See if he's truly found the harbinger as he claims."

Ah. His eyes widened at the mention of yet another sibling —though, one destined to ruin the world and all who inhabited it. Oddly enough, he'd almost forgotten about her, his mysterious half-sister whom Marcus claimed to know the whereabouts of.

This woman didn't seem to be one of Liva's spawn, meaning her interest in his sister stemmed from one purpose.

"Why?" he asked.

"Curiosity." The woman made a low sound in her throat he sensed wasn't a laugh. "And to confirm a suspicion held by my employer."

Logan's eyes narrowed. "Liva?" It was a hunch. If his mother wanted to track down her own daughter, Logan doubted she'd need his help. Still, she was about the evilest bitch he knew.

Who else would want the harbinger of doom?

If she recognized the name, the woman gave nothing away. "No." She stood taller and ran a hand down the front of her black, two-piece suit. It consisted of a tight, low-cut blazer and a dangerously short skirt. A pair of blood-red heels completed the look, but Logan knew better than to underestimate her. She kept her hands at her sides as if used to wielding a weapon, and no lone woman would enter a place like this without either backup, or the skill to render fear moot.

"I come to you on behalf of an organization called Protectors of Dawn. Have you heard of it?"

"No." Though he could guess their intentions well enough. Some cult intent on finding the harbinger. Surprisingly, they were a dime a dozen these days, though he hadn't sought them out.

Doom and gloom weren't really his thing. Neither was betrayal.

Though, when push came to shove, a man didn't have many morals to cling to while in prison.

"We are a collective dedicated to preventing any of the events foreseen in the old prophecies from coming to fruition."

The "old prophecies." That was a hell of a way to refer to the collection of ancient rumors and myths that seemed to predict the conception and birth of him and his siblings. Frankly, Logan wasn't a fan of gossip and speculation. He hadn't even bothered to read any of the published texts and wasn't keen to start now.

Even if his brain seemed determined to replay what could have been a vision of said apocalypse taking place.

"And why the hell do I care?" he asked.

"Because murder is a serious crime," the woman replied, her tone curt. "Without accepting our little offer, you might as well get comfortable here, because you won't ever leave. If you survive your sentencing, that is. Attempted theft, angering a daemon lord, larceny, and lest we don't forget, killing the guard who got in your way. You have quite the charges stacked up against you."

The sad part? He couldn't refute a single one. Evidence wasn't a big factor in the daemonic justice system. Just money and power—two things he sorely lacked.

So, he saved his breath and sighed, knowing when to accept defeat.

"Let's say I find her," he said cautiously. "Then what? Wind her up and watch the world go boom?"

"No." The woman's grin fell flat. "You merely prick her with your blade and prevent the apocalypse from ever taking place."

"What blade?" Logan replied evasively. Alarm shot down his spine, warning that this woman already knew damn well what the weapon in question meant to him.

"Your enchanted blade," she said, displaying straight, white teeth, no fangs in sight. She wasn't a Raeth, but she didn't ooze the sensuality of a Shael. A Vaer, perhaps? That breed sure loved to cut bargains and deals. And excelled in utilizing blackmail. "Krall, I think you call it? We've kept it safe, if that's what you're worried about," she added.

Logan already knew as much. Krall wasn't a normal knife. He could sense its presence like an extra limb, somewhere restrained, but close by. While he didn't know much about the weapon his mother gifted him as a child, he knew that whenever it was out of his possession, he felt...

Vulnerable.

"One little cut should do the trick," the woman continued. "After that, freedom is yours to enjoy. Should you fail... You will suffer in a way that makes your stint here look like a lovely vacation on a beach in Mexico."

An oddly specific location in the mortal realm he'd only heard of through rumors.

"And what's to stop me from running off?" he asked.

"Oh, you can try," she murmured. "In fact, I hope you do. Then you and I will become much better acquainted. I've heard that Shaels can withstand immense amounts of torture—" She flicked her gaze along his bloodied, battered frame, and he swore her grin widened. "I assure you you won't like what I have in mind."

"I'll take your word for it," he replied. Instead of a Vaer, she had to be a Haeth—a rare breed, rumored to master hellfire. They were also known to be sexy, sadistic, and prone to hinting at untold devastation should one refuse their demands. Logan wasn't inclined to find out if the stories were true.

"Sweetheart, get me out of here, and I'll do whatever the fuck you want me to do."

And he'd worry about the consequences later. A life like his didn't leave much room for reliance on a moral compass.

Maybe in another world, he'd hesitate before throwing two of his siblings under the bus.

At the moment, they weren't the ones in prison.

It wasn't every day that a daemon wished he were back in Hell. Maybe his reoccurring nightmare was a sign of homesickness rather than a grim warning?

Writhing at the center of chaos and hellfire was right where he belonged. Despite the tiny matter of being on parole from daemonic prison, things were simpler in the other realm. A lot of the shitty atmosphere and lawlessness were left up to the imagination. On the other hand, mortals were so damn literal they needed a sign to remind them of everything.

How fast to go.

How fast *not* to go.

Unfortunately, they didn't have a billboard proclaiming *Imminent Doom—the Apocalypse is Nigh*, posted along the highway. At least then, the person in front of him wouldn't have been driving so damn slowly.

Annoyed, Logan laid on the horn until the sluggish station wagon sped up, allowing him to pass it. A second later, he turned onto the off-ramp leading to a small town called Meyweather and instantly regretted the drive. *Damn.* Prison had more interesting scenery than these manicured lawns and white-picket fences.

Hell, there didn't even seem to be a bar except for one tiny little pub downtown, which just so happened to be his destination.

With a sigh, he parked and stepped out into the blinding light of midday, unsure what one was meant to do before meeting his long-lost half-brother. Bring flowers? One look at the place confirmed his worst fears—it was painfully, *boringly* mortal.

Marcus had given off *boy scout* vibes during their first official meeting. Apparently, he lived like one too.

Just great. For a second, Logan reconsidered the entire plan —family reunion and secret blackmail and all. Then he froze as the back of his neck prickled with awareness. *Damn.* A glance over his shoulder confirmed his worst suspicions—a shadowy figure stepped from the mouth of a nearby alley, their attention on him.

"Logan," they said in a voice so guttural it resonated through his core.

Out of habit, he reached for the knife he always kept in the pocket of his jeans. There weren't many people out there who knew his name. Scratch that—there weren't many people who knew his name and *didn't* want him dead.

Perhaps all that bullshit about saving the world had been mere pretext to lure him into a trap? Not quite. As the familiar black eyes of the approaching figure caught the light, Logan relaxed. A fraction, anyway.

"Marcus," he greeted, scrambling into a welcoming stance. Hugs weren't his thing, so he settled for a halfhearted shrug. "Long time no see."

"Logan." Marcus merely nodded in response. "It's about damn time you showed up."

Three months had passed since their last meeting, but Logan had spent most of that time in prison, unable to visit anyone, much less his brother. Rather than say as much, he forced a grin. "Nice to see you too."

Marcus grunted.

Logan sighed. As far as reunions went, that was about as sappy as it was going to get. Though, if he *did* want to get sappy, he'd admit that it felt weird standing a few feet from the brother he'd only met a few months ago. Some might say surreal. Until he remembered that the reason for this visit had to do with preventing the end of the world.

Talk about an opportunity for sibling bonding.

"Have a nice drive?" Marcus asked, casually leaning against a brick wall that formed part of a small bistro.

Physically, they could be described as night and day. Marcus, with his long black hair and dark eyes, clearly embodied the latter concept. Crossing his arms over his plain T-shirt, he fixed Logan with an impassive stare. The leather hilt of a knife—nearly identical to Logan's—peeked from the right pocket of his jeans.

"I didn't beat anyone to death in a fit of road rage, if that's what you mean," Logan replied while circling back to his truck. "And look at you, being a good hostess." Wrenching open the passenger-side door, he withdrew a gray duffle and slung it over one shoulder. Inside it were the handful of items he'd salvaged from his time in Hell.

"I hope you know that you'll be cooking your own food," Marcus grumbled. "And I'm not a damn maid, either— you'll be expected to clean up after yourself."

Logan smirked. "Aw! Does this mean no breakfast in bed?"

"You bet your ass it does. Come on." Inclining his head, Marcus started down the narrow sidewalk. "I'll show you around."

"To a drink, I hope," Logan suggested, falling into step behind him.

Fortunately, this section of town seemed slightly more alive than the rest. The street itself contained a plain deli, a vacant lot, and the pub. Along the brick front, a row of wide windows peered into the simple barroom, while a glass door proclaimed the name in cherry red letters—*The Seralis Pub*.

"Nice," Logan said with a nod of appreciation. "Very clever."

The foreign word probably sounded cute to the mortal patrons. Mysterious. Only someone versed in the daemonic tongue could discern the true meaning—*Seralis* was an old word of protection from evil. The big bad, world-ending kind of evil.

Considering their bloodline, they could use all the protection they could get.

Marcus accepted the compliment with a grunt. "You can put your stuff upstairs, I guess," he suggested while opening the door. "*If* you plan on staying..."

Logan shrugged. "It's not like I have anywhere else to go."

Although he had some mortal money saved up, he wasn't exactly in the mood to rent an apartment in some mundane city. As for the daemonic underworld...

Well, he had burned *those* bridges months ago.

Literally.

As if reading his mind, Marcus said, "You're welcome to stay as long as you like. I mean it."

"Thanks." Logan winced as a rare emotion swept over his body. Was that gratitude?

He didn't like it.

Desperate for a distraction, he inspected the decent-sized bar and found himself choking out another rare bit of praise. "This place doesn't look half bad."

The interior was homey enough to set it apart from any other *hole-in-the-wall*. A long bar near the back was surrounded by shelves of liquor, paired with paneled-wood walls and rustic floors.

"Thanks. My apartment's upstairs," Marcus explained while reaching for Logan's duffle. "I'll drop your stuff off, and then—" He let out a heavy breath that conveyed far more than exhaustion. "Then, we'll go see…"

"Her," Logan finished.

He understood his brother's hesitation. The prospect of being reunited with one's long-lost sister—especially when that sister turned out to be the prophesied harbinger of doom—wasn't an everyday occurrence.

Logan, however, harbored another worry he assumed Marcus didn't share—being the one tasked with delivering said harbinger to a cult of daemon hunters who wanted her dead.

Too bad he hadn't brought some champagne, because this was shaping up to be one hell of a family reunion.

She was a doctor, kind of, according to Marcus. Nurse practitioner something or other. Whatever the term, she was an *actual* healer intent on saving people.

Like, for real.

Logan refused to believe it, until they pulled up to a small clinic not far from the pub—a fact he suspected wasn't a coincidence.

"You moved here to keep an eye on her," he said softly, eyeing Marcus, who claimed the passenger's seat.

Marcus nodded. "She's worth protecting."

Logan pretended not to hear that. Instead, he watched the mortals trickle through the glass doors like bees in a hive and tried to ignore his building unease. Out of all of them —his mismatched siblings that he knew of—how strange was it that *she* would be the one to dedicate her life to helping others? *Before* she cast the world into the pits of Hell, of course.

"So, what's the game plan?" he asked. "Go in and say hello? Are hugs off-limits? To be completely honest, I'm not anxious to trigger an apocalypse—"

"She's a good person," Marcus insisted, as he exited the truck. "Try not to judge her by the rumors. Just wait and see for yourself."

"Yeah," Logan grunted. "Sure."

He wasn't really a firm believer in the whole "never judge a book by its cover," thing. As far as he was concerned, if a book had a scary-ass "doom and gloom" looking cover, it was probably a good idea *not* to go peeking inside it.

Or, in his case, turn said book over to a cult of daemon hunters intent on burning every last page.

Still, he tried to keep an open mind as he followed Marcus inside the building. She had grown up mortal…so she couldn't be *all* bad, right? His upbringing had been a bit more unorthodox, and while he may have had his rough edges, he wasn't completely morally bankrupt. Then again, *her* father had been eviler than the devil himself, not to mention their dear old mother wasn't exactly a shining example of goodness, either.

Logan had no idea what to expect. Should he have brought a present? Maybe a "Have fun bringing about the apocalypse," card? Or one that read, "Sorry, in advance, for betraying you."

By the time he followed Marcus into the small waiting room of the clinic, it was too late to turn back. *Trapped*, he thought as the sliding glass doors closed behind him, confining him in a modest lobby enclosed by white walls and plastic-looking furniture.

"Can I help you?" The soft voice drew his attention to the woman standing behind the front desk, and another emotion instantly replaced the unease.

"*You* most certainly can," he replied huskily.

While not the prettiest creature he'd ever seen, the woman had shiny red hair, clear skin, and pink lips that probably tasted as sweet as her smile.

Definitely worth the second glance.

"Logan," he heard Marcus growl in warning. "Knock it off."

As if he could just turn off the hot lust coiling in his belly on demand. He couldn't help it. It was in his blood. Literally.

While their mother had been a witch, he and Marcus had different fathers—each of the daemonic variety. Logan's father had been one-hundred percent Shael—a type of daemon who thrived on…"entertaining" members of the opposite sex.

With deliberate effort, he averted his gaze to the wall *behind* the secretary, instead of the soft mounds shaping the front of her peach sweater.

"Oh, hey Marcus," she said warmly as if noticing the man for the first time. "You here to see—"

"Yes." Marcus nodded. "Is she around?"

From the corner of his eye, Logan saw the secretary shrug.

"I think they left early to help set up. We're having a fundraiser tomorrow night for Daily Peace," she added. "You and your friend are more than welcome to join us. And if he were interested in helping out, I have a brochure right here."

Logan didn't miss the subtle way she said *friend*—all sexy and drawn out. With a dry swallow, he forced himself to read the first line of a poster proclaiming that hand hygiene was "super-duper important" rather than drag his gaze back to visually confirm if the attraction was mutual.

Who was he kidding? Of course, it was.

"Thanks, Rachel," Marcus said. "But, we can't—" His dark eyes cut in Logan's direction. "It wouldn't do good to cause any *trouble*."

Adequately cowed, Logan high-tailed it out of there before he could do something he most likely *wouldn't* regret.

It'd been a while since he'd been laid. Well over a week, he realized with a hint of panic. While that may not have been a source of alarm to anyone else, for him, that marked the beginning of a damn near dry spell. After all, he partly belonged to a race of daemons, whose name in their original tongue actually meant "sex."

Maybe…once Marcus returned to the bar, he might sneak over to properly introduce himself to the buxom, charming Rachel?

"Don't even think about it," Marcus grumbled as if reading his mind. "I'm not having you running around fucking anything that moves. This isn't the damn underworld. You need to be careful. Cause any trouble, and it will be traced right back to me."

"You mean to tell me you've been the paragon of virtue?" Logan tossed back.

Marcus didn't even hesitate before nodding, much to Logan's utter shock. "I've practiced self-control, if that's what you mean," he replied, his tone serious. "While in the mortal realm, I've embraced celibacy. Maybe you should try it?"

Logan flinched. He'd rather manually castrate himself than willingly abstain from sex. Still, he sensed that Marcus hadn't been bullshitting him. While the man seemed uptight to a fault, Logan suspected his restraint had to do more with his nature as a half-Raeth than any moral authority.

That breed was known for going off the deep end when it came to the vices Shaels loved to indulge in. Those drawn to alcohol became alcoholics. Those partial to sex, tended to be ruthless in their pursuit of it, and those with an inclination toward blood… Well, they wound up in the worst daemonic prisons. Apparently, Marcus didn't want to give in to his dark side.

Go figure.

While he had enough tact not to say as much outright, Logan couldn't resist needling him on another topic. "I won't tolerate your racist bullshit," he said with a scoff. "Fuck anything that moves? I do have *standards,* you know."

A lie. Anything that had two legs, boobs, and a pulse was pretty much fair game, but he did have his preferences. Preferences that the little Rachel seemed more than fit to satisfy.

"You damn Shaels never know when to quit," Marcus said as they exited into the bright light of midday. "Just remember to rein yourself in around *her.*"

That's right, Logan remembered with a frown. Their sister, the future *Ms. Apocalypse* in question, had no idea about their world. Her world. As far as she was concerned, she was an innocent little mortal, adopted by human parents.

"You still haven't told her," Logan suspected. "After all this time, you still haven't told her who she really is." He wasn't sure whether to be pissed or relieved. On the one hand, she wouldn't know anything about daemon hunters or how to spot them.

Then again, she might accidentally end the world in the meantime. Sooner or later, she'd be in for one hell of a rude awakening, and he wasn't inclined to stick around for the fireworks.

"Not yet." Marcus had the nerve to shrug. "It hasn't exactly come up."

"Have you ever tried—'Hey, long lost sis, I'm your brother, and your real mother is an evil bitch—I mean *witch*. By the way, your real father was a daemon eviler than evil itself, and you, my dear, are destined to destroy the world'?"

Marcus didn't even dignify that with a response. "As far as she's concerned, I'm just her long-lost cousin four times removed on her adopted father's side—and that's just how it needs to stay."

"Humph." Logan doubted that would be the case for long, but he had enough sense to keep his mouth shut. Marcus might have been on his best behavior now, but *his* father was a Raeth daemon—and that race wasn't exactly known for its patience.

Or its tolerance of betrayal.

"Come on. The rec center's not far from the pub," Marcus said, before climbing back into Logan's truck. "Park there, and we can walk."

And then, he'd finally meet Little Miss Apocalypse in the flesh.

MINUTES LATER, they stood before a building a few blocks away from Marcus' bar. A small sign on the spacious front lawn read, "Meyweather Community Center," and the landscaping looked charming and welcoming. Not exactly the venue Logan could picture anyone throwing a party at.

Or the backdrop for his first meeting with the harbinger of death and destruction.

One step inside proved his first suspicion wrong, at least. Decorations transformed the interior into a relatively festive space. People rushed to and fro carrying supplies, and at the center of the commotion stood a pint-sized woman barking out orders.

"Please tell me that isn't her," Logan muttered to Marcus.

His brother followed his gaze and shook his head. "No. Not her."

Logan didn't know whether to be relieved or not. Though, if she *weren't* his half-sister, he couldn't explain why this woman captured his attention so thoroughly. The fact that she held herself with all the poise of a daemon overlord might have played a role.

He'd always preferred the domineering types.

"I need those banners hung," she commanded, her icy tone a harsh contrast to the cheerful atmosphere. "And the programs need to be laid out, *exactly* as I demonstrated. Understand, Robbie?" She focused her full attention on a man who flinched beneath the scrutiny.

Logan didn't blame him. He—and most of the workers— sported a lime-green shirt with "Daily Peace Outreach Program" printed in black across the front. Though peace wasn't the word he'd apply to the current mood.

Robbie and his comrades looked oppressed more than anything, ruthlessly stewarded by a woman as intimidating as she was short.

The longer he observed her, the more Logan was perplexed by *why* he felt compelled to stare in the first place. She wasn't overtly sexy, or even his usual type. Her jet-black hair was pulled back severely from a plain face, crowned by two intense gray eyes, and she was so pale, Logan would have guessed she was a vampire if it weren't for the fact that she stood directly in a pool of sunlight spilling from a large bay window.

Her outfit didn't help to displace the frosty exterior. The sweater and crisply-tailored pants—both in a foreboding shade of ebony—seemed special ordered from "Bitches 'R Us."

"I gotcha, Serana," the unfortunate Robbie mumbled before scurrying off.

"Good. We can't afford any more delays." With that, Serana turned on her heel, leaving her minions to snap into action.

Damn. Logan exhaled. He'd always believed his *mother* to be the pinnacle of the phrase "cracking the whip," but this mortal seemed on par with her in the evil general department. That should have been a red flag if there ever were one. Still...he couldn't resist the impulse to follow her, monumental task to save the world be damned.

"Don't get into any trouble," he heard Marcus grumble. "I'll find her."

Logan nodded, though he was already fully focused on his quarry. The ice princess had moved to a corner of the room and was now crouched before a stack of boxes. As he crept up behind her, he couldn't help but notice how nicely she filled out those hideous pants. It almost made up for the fact that her restrictive clothing revealed little else.

"I take it you're in charge around here?" he asked by way of greeting.

She inclined her head and took him in with an impassive sweep of those silver eyes. When they widened, he smirked, unsurprised—his body tended to have that effect on the opposite sex.

"Deliveries go in the back," she murmured, turning away.

Logan blinked. "I'm Logan," he blurted. "And you are?"

"*Busy*, Logan."

Her tone threw him off, polite and cold at the same damn time. Even stranger, she seemed to be completely uninterested in him. Which was just plain…weird.

A jolt of unexpected self-consciousness lanced through his chest, and he inspected his jeans and T-shirt with a critical eye. Had those months in prison damaged his allure?

Then he remembered how many times he'd been laid since then and shook off the doubt. Obviously, she hadn't gotten a good enough look at him the first time. Luckily for her, he was more than happy to oblige for a second.

"I'm new in town," he went on while maneuvering to stand directly in front of her. "I was hoping that maybe someone might be able to show me around?"

The last thing he wanted to do was take a tour around Dullsville, the mortal edition, but the lie gave him an excuse to keep talking. Which seemed very important to do suddenly.

She couldn't have looked at him head-on and *not* be drooling.

It just wasn't possible.

As if reading his mind, she lifted her head, and Logan waited, confident that any minute her eyes would turn soft and languid.

"This is a private function," she snapped instead, apparently un-wooed. "Not a bordello, which is exactly where you need to head if you're after what I think you are."

His mouth dropped open. *What. The. Hell?*

"Are we done here?" The woman smoothed one hand along her hair while brandishing an object casually held in the other—a small box cutter. He didn't miss the unspoken warning. Maybe Marcus and those daemon hunters had gotten their intel wrong? This mortal seemed more than willing to end the world one stab wound at a time, starting with him. "Or do I need to call security?"

Her tone snapped him from his daze.

"Call them," he taunted, taking a step closer. "I've always liked having an audience."

Shock ignited that frosty expression. After dolling out her orders, it seemed she wasn't used to someone talking back. "Excuse me?"

"You heard me." Chuckling, Logan stood closer, gazing down at her upturned face. So, the mortal wanted to play hard to get?

He could play too.

"*You're* the one who suggested exhibition. It's my favorite game."

She kind of looked cute when she was startled. Her eyes widened, and the expression displaced some of that frosty air.

For all of five seconds. The next, her eyes flashed silver, and her lips pressed into a thin, stern line. "I don't know who the hell you are or what you're playing at, but I'll give you until the count of *one* to back off. *One*—"

"Or what?" Logan replied. Much like his daemon nature, he couldn't help it. He had always had a rebellious streak—and a weakness for women who didn't fall for the usual bullshit pickup lines. She tempted him to get creative, and he couldn't resist lowering his gaze to her chest as he came up with a new proposition. "Though, I'll be honest and admit that I really wouldn't want anyone else to see you all twisted in my bedsheets—"

Zap!

Pain shot through his arm, drawing a grunt from his lips. Dazed, he glanced down, surprised to find a bead of scarlet smeared over his forearm. His blood. The sight shocked the hell out of him—*almost* as much as the tiny woman, hissing like an alley cat, still holding that damn box cutter in a clenched fist, did.

He couldn't believe it…

She actually cut him.

"Obviously, you can't comprehend English," she snarled, rising to her feet, "so I'll make this clear—stay the hell away from me, or next time, I won't just go for your *arm*—"

"Serana?"

They turned in unison to find a tall woman approaching them—though Logan figured they stiffened for very different reasons.

"Mirabelle," the woman, Serana, said at the same time Logan croaked, "Liva."

Holy hell. The fact that his mother was way too much of a haughty bitch to ever set foot in a mortal hovel was the only reason he didn't draw his knife. That and the realization that the woman's eyes were a calming shade of blue rather than haunting gold.

Marcus stood behind her, and Logan saw him mouth, "It's her." Then it clicked. This woman with hair a blazing shade of yellow was *her*—their sister.

So, their mother had named her Mirabelle. Logan struggled to hide his disgust. While the name might have sounded pretty in the mortal tongue, in the daemonic language, it had a more sinister meaning—one so fucked up he didn't even want to think about it. Instead, he drew himself to his full height and observed the woman prophesied to bring doom to the world and all who inhabited it.

His first observation was…she didn't *look* evil. Her smile seemed genuinely kind, bright enough to rival the ribbons of sunlight streaming across the floor, with no hint of malice whatsoever. Hell, Logan was willing to suspect that she couldn't destroy a *fly*, let alone the universe.

"You must be Logan!" she exclaimed with bubbly excitement.

He could only stare as she rushed forward to throw her arms around his neck. Thankfully, he had enough sense to extend his wounded limb to prevent any blood from staining her cream-colored sweater.

"Marcus told me so much about you!" Mirabelle went on as she pulled back, oblivious to his awkward position. "How weird is it? That I've had family out there all along who I've never met?"

"I… What?" Logan glanced at his brother, who just shrugged. In the six seconds he'd been harassing the icy Serana, had Marcus spilled the beans already? If he *had*, then for someone who had just discovered that her whole life had been one massive lie, Mirabelle looked peachy keen.

"About us being cousins," she explained, laughing. "When Marcus told me, I'll admit I was a little mind-blown. I didn't even know my dad had family from Oregon."

"Oregon?" Logan croaked. Obviously, his brother had gone all out in stretching the truth.

From over Mirabelle's shoulder, he saw Marcus shrug—*just go with it.*

"Yeah," he blurted, regaining his senses. "When Marcus invited me out here, I tearfully left the family horse farm straight away…so eager to meet my fancy new cousin from the big city."

So maybe that was laying it on a bit thick, but that was what Marcus got for such a stupid lie. Logan was satisfied to see his brother flinch, though Mirabelle didn't even seem to smell the bullshit he'd just thrown at her.

Serana, however, glanced at him sharply, and Logan felt impressed despite their growing animosity—obviously, she was not as naïve as his newfound "cousin."

"It's nice to meet you, finally, Mirabelle," he said. "Really… Nice."

His hand twitched toward Krall—though he figured it wouldn't be polite to ask straight away if he could draw just a drop of her blood with his ancient daemon blade. Certainly not with Marcus watching.

"I mean… I know I was adopted, but it's weird how much we look alike."

"Huh?" Logan's focus whipped right back to Mirabelle, who inspected him, an eyebrow raised. She had a point. They had both taken after Liva in their coloring and facial features. By merely meeting her in person, had he blown Marcus' ruse apart?

He looked to his brother, who seemed unfazed by the resemblance.

"I think it's just a sign that we were meant to meet," he said, his tone unrelentingly calm.

"Yeah, I guess," Mirabelle gushed. "And I've always wanted to go to the Midwest. What kind of horses did you keep?"

"Uh…" Logan muttered a half-hearted, "big ones," and it was Marcus' turn to snicker.

Mirabelle laughed as if he'd made a joke. "You know, it's wonderful that you guys happened to show up when you did. We could really use the help—" She broke off abruptly, her gaze on Logan's arm. "Oh gosh! You're bleeding! What happened?"

"Nothing," Logan insisted, gently pulling his arm away.

Mirabelle shook her head. "It looks deep. You should still get it looked at…" As she fell silent, Logan suspected she had finally noticed the box-cutter-wielding woman standing beside him. "Serana? Is everything okay?"

"It's nothing," Serana said. Though, Logan could tell that it took considerable effort for her to keep up the hard-ass act in the face of Mirabelle's disappointment. "This is a community center, Mirabelle. Not somewhere to host your damn family reunion. Let me know when you're ready to get back to work."

With that, she turned on her heel—but not before tossing Logan a little goodbye present. The box cutter clattered across the floor to strike his shoe.

Damn. "What the hell is her deal?" Logan heard himself grumble. The enterprising part of his brain wasn't too offended, though. She had more balls with a blade than he did in Marcus' presence. Maybe he should rope her into his scheme? His freedom would be earned within seconds.

If he didn't stab her beforehand out of vengeance.

Sure, he had all but propositioned her in the rudest way possible, but it wasn't his fault. Mortal or daemon—no one ever turned him down. Eyes narrowed, he watched Serana march across the rec center, snapping at whoever had the misfortune of crossing her path.

"Her family, the Blakes, used to own the clinic—not to mention half the town before her father died," Mirabelle murmured wistfully. Her soft voice was the only force capable of dragging Logan back from the sudden lust-tinged rage that rose up as he glanced down at his now freely-bleeding arm.

"Her father died not long ago, but she still helps out as our accountant, and she runs Daily Peace, the addiction program. I don't know what we'd do without her. She's kind of..." Mirabelle sighed as if fishing for the right word. "Prickly—though for a good reason after everything she's been through."

Which Logan assumed was a polite way of saying a total bitch. He still couldn't believe she had managed to cut him. Draw *his* blood. There were fully-grown daemons who couldn't say the same.

"Come on," Mirabelle said, suddenly looping her slender arm through his. "Let's go. Marcus told me you just got here. I can show you around town before you turn in."

"I'll clear my schedule," Marcus chimed in.

Reluctantly, Logan allowed her to steer him through the door, and contemplated "accidentally" scratching her with Krall then and there. To his immense irritation, something else distracted him from the possibility of limitless freedom —a dark-haired woman with piercing gray eyes sneaking glances at him from her corner of the room.

Barely an hour in the mortal realm, and already things were starting to seem way more interesting than he'd initially thought.

Not that he would have very long to enjoy it.

THREE

The day spent with Mirabelle had been…strange, to say the least.

Eternally cheerful, she took them to the park, and the public library, all while chattering on about the history of the town.

"It's a typical small town all in all," she claimed, though she had no idea just how *foreign* it seemed to Logan.

He had been in Hell way too long. Where were the rowdy bars and the shadowy dwellings? Where were the fire and brimstone? Some chaos, maybe?

The unofficial tour merely cemented how urgently he needed to complete his mission and go. The town of Meyweather was way too idyllic for his liking. Even as a kid, he had always preferred a gritty, volatile environment. It was easier to be on guard that way, and never get caught unaware. All this peace and quiet seemed…unnatural.

Though, Mirabelle obviously loved the place she called home.

After only a few hours, there wasn't a doubt in Logan's mind that she was good. *Truly* good—the type of person who didn't deserve the fate some damn twisted prophecy saddled her with. And, the type of person who might be destroyed by the knowledge of who—or in this case, what—she really was.

Maybe, Marcus wasn't so stupid for keeping the truth from her.

Once night fell, and they returned to the bar, another emotion gradually replaced the awe of seeing his sister for the first time.

Irritation.

Perched on a stool at the counter, Logan poured himself a glass and tried to drown his annoyance the way he did most problems—with liquor. It didn't work. After several shots, he still felt pissed and a little horny. The anger he chalked up to the task weighing on his mind. As for the arousal. Well, that had a more obvious cause, though he loathed admitting as much...

Serana Blake.

Scowling, he eyed the nick in his arm. It still hurt, but nowhere near as much as his pride did. Injured by a human, the indecency of it. To numb both pains, he tossed back another shot, slammed the empty glass down, and braced his hands against the counter.

Stewing over the insult would help nothing. He needed to take action. How to right such a grievous wrong?

"You can't kill her, you know." The voice accompanied the massive hand that swooped down to snatch his glass away before he had the chance to take another swig. "Serana," Marcus added, meeting his stare boldly. "I saw how you hounded her. You're lucky that all she did was cut you."

Before Logan could react, Marcus stole his bottle too.

Damn.

"I know that," he spat. Though, in all honesty, that rule had become a little fuzzy.

Mortals, with their damn innocence, fear of the unknown, and fervent imaginations, were off-limits to his kind. For now, at least.

Considering that the world was being swallowed whole by an evil most humans couldn't imagine in their nightmares, who knew how long the unofficial truce would last? As order broke to chaos, Logan figured humans would soon become fair game.

In the meantime?

He would just have to contend with punishing Serana Blake another way, and he could be creative when he wanted to be. Admittedly, it'd been a while since he'd met a woman who demanded such ingenuity.

"If I'd known the women out here were feistier than the ones in Hell, I would have come a long damn time ago," he snapped.

"What have you been up to, anyway?" Marcus asked, an eyebrow raised. "Last time I saw you, Haedyn didn't seem very welcoming."

The man didn't even know half of it. The last time they'd met, Logan had an arrest warrant hanging overhead. Rather than play a round of show and tell, Logan shrugged. "Last time I saw you, wasn't your daddy in tow?"

He made a show of eyeing the empty bar room. Unsurprisingly, the massive, ancient Raeth Marcus had called Atiernan wasn't in view.

"I take it, the mortal plane isn't his scene?"

"No," Marcus replied. "Though I take it he would have fared better than you have. He at least seems housebroken when it comes to women. I told you to *rein it in*—and don't walk around my bar like that, either. Or, at least take a cold shower. You'll scare the customers."

At first, Logan assumed he was referring to the bloodstains on his shirt. Or perhaps the enchanted daemon blade sticking from his front pocket? But then he shifted, feeling his zipper scrape against another…weapon.

Oh.

That was the problem with being part Shael. Their desire for sex was triggered by pain—*intense* pain—and Serana, intentionally or not, had topped the lid off his threshold with that jab from her blade. Though, to be fair, after being tortured for months in a shitty prison, anyone would be on edge. Sure, most wouldn't get a hard-on in the process, but that was what came with the daemonic heritage.

Torture, physical pain, and all those delicious little agonies, broke the minds of other men—mortals and daemons alike. Shaels worked a little differently. The torture had been just as painful for him, but in a very different way…

By cutting him, Serana had unknowingly released a Pandora's box. Annoyed, he dragged a finger along the cut's edge and popped the digit into his mouth. The salty taste of blood took some of the edge off, though nowhere near enough to let him think rationally.

"Can't kill her," he repeated, bringing his fist down hard over the counter.

"No," Marcus agreed, appearing beside him to wipe at a drop of spilled liquor. "No torture either," he added before Logan could even voice the suggestion. "No beating, or threatening, or brutalizing. Anything you do would most likely be traced back to *me*, and I've worked too damn hard making a name for myself in this town to have you fuck it all up."

Logan scowled. "Then why invite me here?"

Marcus raised an eyebrow. "You really want to know? Because you *are* a fuck up. Like me. Like anyone else who has the misfortune of calling Liva their mother. I understand that pain better than anyone. You belong here. It's about damn time you realized that."

Logan frowned. Marcus actually sounded genuine, which just…puzzled him. Feelings were a new experience, all things considered.

"How did you find her?" Logan asked, clearing his throat. "You know who—"

"You can say her name," Marcus said over him. "*Mirabelle.* Poetic, you must give our mother points for that."

Poetic or sadistic. Logan didn't care to decide.

"How did you find her?" he reiterated. "A million daemon hunters and religious zealots, and *you* alone managed to find her. How?"

Marcus chuckled. "You may be part Shael, but I'm part Raeth. Fucking is your forte. Tracking is mine."

"Touché," Logan replied. Most Raeths tended to be mercenaries for a reason. His kind? Well, someone had to run the strip clubs, even in Hell. "What are you planning? Keep an eye on her in case she decides to trigger an apocalypse?"

"No," Marcus said. "I plan on keeping an eye on everyone in this town. No one will harm Mirabelle if I have any say in it. Not until we know for sure."

"What?" Logan felt his eyes widen. "You think it could be another lucky sister? How many of us are there, by the way?"

He'd met only one other brother in addition to Marcus—a daemon-hunting asshole named Jace, whom he wouldn't mind never meeting again. Still, he suspected there were far more half-daemons running around, wreaking havoc, born of Liva.

Marcus shrugged. "I found you easily enough."

"You didn't answer my question," Logan pointed out. "Why? Worried I might track them down one by one and put us all out of our misery?"

"No. I'm worried that a family reunion too soon might tip the scales in the wrong direction. Think what you want, but I'm not exactly in a hurry for the world to end."

Logan scowled. "So that's your motive. You want to become *domesticated*, for lack of a better word."

Marcus raised an eyebrow. "I want *peace*, if that's what you want to call it. You seem to want the same. Why else would you finally come out here to meet me? It's not as if the daemon world has treated you any better than the mortal one."

Logan shrugged—he had a point. "I needed a change of scenery."

"No," Marcus said with a guttural laugh. "You needed to keep a low profile on account of half of Hell wanting you dead. What? You thought that just because I'm on the outside, I'm not aware of the rumors? I know that you did something foolish enough to land in prison. You don't have to explain—I don't want to know. Frankly, I'm surprised you got out in one piece."

Logan sighed. Surprisingly, he wasn't so shocked Marcus knew. Though, he suspected his brother was only aware of *half* of the story regarding his unofficial jailbreak—otherwise, he'd never let him anywhere near Mirabelle.

"It wasn't as bad as it sounds," he said halfheartedly. "Let's just say I tried to 'borrow' an artifact from a powerful daemon lord. Got caught. Prison wasn't fun, so I cut a deal to save my skin. It's all on the up and up."

Minus the minor detail of someone dying in the aftermath, and what that artifact happened to be. Prison was supposed to make a man regret his poor decisions, right? In the weeks since his stint in Arcaneum, his most prevalent thought had been a pressing need to try again. Find it, whatever it was. Because if he didn't…

Damn, he wasn't sure, but he was willing to try anything to stop the nightmares plaguing him nearly every damn night. The ones of the world burning…

With him at the center. Though, he figured Marcus didn't need to know every last detail.

"Either way, the person who hired me must have sold me out," he said dismissively. "I guess we inherited our knack for making friends from our mother."

"Don't even mention her." Marcus spat on the floor as if to banish the mere mention of Liva—even daemons had their superstitions. "Look… I don't need to know what you've gotten yourself into. Just know that I've taken the proper precautions. As long as you're in Meyweather, no one from the other realm can find you here, but in return, I ask that you lay low. No orgies. No underground sex dungeons. No—"

"No fun," Logan finished with a grimace. "I get it. But what do you mean by 'precautions?' You know a witch? A warlock? Last I heard, Raeths can track, but they can't cast spells."

His brother chuckled and tossed his rag into the sink. "I stay out of your business, and you stay out of mine. Though, keep in mind that my protection goes both ways. Consider everyone in this town off-limits—*including* Serana Blake. She's had it hard enough without having to take shit from a Shael."

"Hard how?" Logan asked. Though hell, it wasn't like him to be curious about someone's past. Certainty, not a mortal's.

"In a manner of speaking, she's been through hell," Marcus said with a sigh. "Just stay away from her. That's my one stipulation while you're here. No meddling with the locals."

Whatever Serana had been through, it had to be bad enough to make a Raeth uneasy. Which unsettled Logan for a reason he couldn't name. He wasn't curious enough to disobey Marcus' boundary, however. A part of him was still in awe of having a brother in the first place. Being an outcast had been his primary character trait for so damn long…

It was hard to be original in a realm where some daemons could spit fire or drink blood, after all—but being a half-witch was enough to slap any child with an infamous stigma since birth. There was a time when he wore that "otherness" as a badge of honor, and a license to keep everyone else at arm's length. Who needed friends when your very existence was considered a gross abomination? As it turned out, he wasn't so special after all.

Just a tool devised by Liva for only God knew what purpose.

Mirabelle, despite her horrific fate, had gotten the best outcome of Liva's known children. She'd had a family around. Love. Logan had been lucky to make it out of diapers in one piece. Horrific upbringing aside, he'd learned that not all daemons were evil, ruthless bastards desperate to kill anyone with a drop of mortal blood. Some, like Marcus apparently, wanted to live in harmony with the humans —*protect* them. That superhero bullshit.

While he wasn't into murder and torture like his more full-blooded daemon brethren, Logan wasn't so inclined to play nice with the rest of the universe. As far as he was concerned, humans were only good for two things—one was getting in the damn way during daemon wars, and the other…

"I could always sleep with her?" He asked the question offhandedly, but was as surprised at himself as Marcus seemed to be.

Serana Blake wasn't exactly his type—that being lusty, busty, and blond. She wasn't ugly, though. *Oh no.* He pictured that slender form and felt his mouth water. While small, her body would be soft and moldable in his hands. In fact…

Even the thought of how those hard gray eyes would widen in shock, as he kissed her was…

Gritting his teeth, he gripped the edge of the bar for balance. He wanted her, alright. A reaction that was partly thanks to his dear old dad—only a Shael daemon could go from hatred to lust in five seconds.

"Damn it, Logan." Marcus slammed a shot glass in front of him, brimming with a clear liquid. "Maybe you *do* need this after all."

Logan downed the drink without a word. Like gasoline, the fiery liquid burned a trail down his throat.

"You can't fuck her either," Marcus said crassly, before refilling his glass. "I don't want you leaving a trail of broken hearts around this town. Not while I'm here."

Too damn bad, Logan thought. Sex was as much a part of his nature as breathing was to humans, along with a healthy fear of commitment. While this town certainly had its share of buxom beauties, he was more than happy to start with Serana.

"I'm going," he announced, setting his shot glass down. The pub was closed, so there was no one else to watch as he drew himself to his full height, trying to ignore the bulge brushing uncomfortably against his zipper.

"No, you're *not*," Marcus growled from behind the bar. "I told you—I'm not cleaning up your mess."

"It's a good thing then that you aren't my fucking babysitter. Besides, there won't be a mess to clean up," Logan tossed back—which was a big ass lie.

There was *always* a mess. Usually with the throwing of some heavy objects involved. While Shaels loved a good time, he made sure to convey that he was into one-night stands —only.

Some women were fine with that. Others pretended to be, only to freak out later. Thus came the importance of one of the few rules he lived by—never sleep with the same woman twice. Ever.

If things got a little *messy* with the icy Serana, then so be it. For cutting him, she fucking deserved it.

"I'll be good," he promised—another bald-faced lie, but he headed for the door before Marcus could rush after him. "I'm just going to…take a walk."

"A walk," Marcus echoed.

Logan nodded. A walk straight to Serana Blake. Then, in the morning, he'd find Mirabelle, accomplish his task, and be back in Hell by nightfall.

It wasn't an ideal way of handling things where Marcus was concerned, but probably the best method in the end.

He didn't do romantic relationships, so why not add familial ones to the list?

One thing he *did* excel in, however, was revenge. Blood was a vital substance to a Shael, allowing them to track anyone foolish enough to draw it—which meant he had an invisible map right to Serana Blake.

And he fully intended to return the favor.

FOUR

"Damn!" Serana hissed as her thumb caught the edge of the poster she was attempting to pin to the wall. While it stung like a bitch, the cut overall was no longer than her pinky nail.

She would live.

Still, she let loose another curse for the hell of it. What a day. If she were prone to dwelling in pessimism, she might even rethink her five years of narcotics sobriety. God, she needed sleep, and maybe a cold shower. Not only was she stuck in the community center, busting her ass decorating for the fundraiser tomorrow, but she'd been hit on by some asshole with a superiority complex.

A hot asshole. It felt important to emphasize that part. Mirabelle's so-called cousin Logan had been…gorgeous. Breathtaking even, with molten green eyes, the stuff of which most women's fantasies were made—the dark and juicy kind involving ripped bodices and crumpled bedsheets.

Not that Serana was into that sort of kink. Regardless, even she could admit she found it hard to stare at the bastard head-on. His unusual interest in *her*, however, instantly put her on guard. Though, just *maybe*…she had overreacted a little?

Who could blame her? The bastard certainly knew how to make an entrance. Even the men in his orbit had stopped to stare, though for different reasons. Guys were like dogs, after all, always competing for the top spot.

Which, the asshole, Logan seemed to think was on top of *her*. An assumption he had made crudely, with a bold suggestion that still made her cheeks flame.

No one could blame her for cutting him, either. As if being new in town was an excuse for being a pig.

Unfortunately, Mirabelle, the group cheerleader, seemed to think so. Once she and her suffocating good cheer had left, the others had followed suit, with one lame excuse after the other, leaving Serana to finish the work alone.

Like always.

The day someone else pulled their fair share around here would be the day she died—and the "work" would most likely be the removal of her dead body after she collapsed, exhausted, in her own office.

Who needed help, anyway? Alone, she had almost finished hanging the banners, but there were still the tables to organize, and programs to arrange…

Damn it! One stupid paper cut shouldn't have slowed her down so much.

Suck it up, she scolded herself. Then she popped the burning finger into her mouth to squash the pain. *You can cry about it later.* One-handed, she tried to arrange the poster again, only to flinch as a shadow fell over her.

"You missed a spot."

The guttural voice made her throat go dry, and she spun around so quickly she nearly fell off the chair she stood on. Luckily, a firm grip came from nowhere to keep her from losing her balance. A *big* hand, she realized with a gulp. One endowed with thick fingers that threatened to brush her stomach from beneath the hem of her sweater.

Because, of course, the bastard caught her by the waist.

"Don't touch me," she spat, scrambling back until she hit the wall. She blinked twice just to make sure she wasn't hallucinating the man in front of her. That old saying seemed fitting in this instance—speak of the devil, and he shall appear. "How did you even get in here?"

God, it was as if her thoughts really had summoned him, right from the pits of sexy, asshole Hell.

"I didn't mean to startle you." Logan chuckled, his eyes glowing in the semi-darkness.

Was it past sunset already? Sure enough, Serana glanced at the windows and despaired at the sight of the pitch-black sky beyond them. The only light at all came from a sputtering fixture in the ceiling. Trust none of those quitters to have thought to turn on the main lights for her.

Whatever. She didn't need them, and she certainly didn't need to risk criminal charges by committing another accidental stabbing with a box cutter.

"This is a private venue," she replied coldly. "I don't know how you got in here, but you need to leave." Turning her back on Logan, she continued to readjust the banner as if his presence didn't bother her.

It did. He was too close. She didn't miss how his fingers lingered as they withdrew from her waist, either. Cringing, she tried like hell to keep her voice steady.

"What do you want? Mirabelle isn't here."

"I came to apologize," he said. "Though, I figured that *you* wouldn't."

Serana scoffed. "Apologize for what?"

It wasn't until she looked over and saw the splotch of dried blood on his shirt that she realized he had a point.

"I'm sorry," she blurted. "I didn't mean..."

Her voice failed in the face of his smile. Pearly white teeth shone brightly against his tanned skin. Paired with the heated look in those green eyes, the grin held an alarming edge.

"Don't worry about it," he said with a shrug. "But your apology would mean a lot more if you came down and said it to my face."

"Not a chance," Serana hissed—the moment of guilt was over. Angrily, she turned back to the wall and jabbed the corner of the banner to the firm surface, not caring if it was even or not. Without turning around, she reached back for the tape…

Only to gape as Logan ripped off a piece and secured the poster before she could so much as blink.

"There," he murmured, his voice like honey. "Perfect."

"It's crooked," Serana snapped, inching back as quickly as the precarious balance of the chair would allow her. "It looks horrible," she added, just to rub it in.

It would have to do, though. She was far too tired to fix it, and there was still so much left to be done. Her heart sank at the thought of how many stupid banners needed to be hung.

Unless Logan planned to be busy while berating her, she didn't need the distraction. "I really don't have time for this, so if you don't intend to make yourself useful—"

"Move over."

Before she could react, he nudged her off the chair and righted the banner without breaking a sweat.

With his height, he managed to hang the poster higher than she had as well as a hell of a lot straighter. All without getting up on the damn chair or even straining to the tips of his toes.

How tall *was* he? *Six feet? Seven?* Certainly, tall enough to dwarf her—though that wasn't much of a feat when she stood at a solid 5'3".

"Do you have a white knight complex?" she muttered, observing his handiwork with a frown. Most of her annoyance stemmed from pure jealousy—the bastard had done in five seconds what it had taken her almost twenty minutes to achieve.

"No," he replied, surprising her by the heat in his tone. "Just a *perfectionist* complex."

He glanced at her then, and she shivered. His eyes were so damn green, and he was so…massive. Despite the white T-shirt he wore, she could tell the guy was ripped, with sturdy shoulders to kill for.

Snap out of it! She struggled to focus. "*You're* a p-perfection-ist? Color me skeptical."

"I am," Logan insisted, taking a step back from the wall, where the "Welcome to the Meyweather Clinic Fund Rais-er," banner hung above a water fountain. As he moved, she fought to keep her gaze from sliding down to the firm rump shaping the back of those blue jeans.

God, she was going insane…

"But only when it comes to certain things."

Before she could help it, her mind began to question what those "certain things" could be. Crumpled bed sheets and harsh pants were just part of it.

"Well, thank you," she gritted out from between clenched teeth. "But, you can leave now—"

"Do you have anything else that needs to be done?"

The genuine offer threw her off, long enough for the meaningful silence to say more than her hasty refusal did. "I don't need—"

"What else? I have the time."

She hesitated for another second before common sense took over. "Those still need to be hung." She pointed to the printed banners stacked near the table.

Logan had already moved. In a fluid motion of tanned skin, he hefted a box over his shoulder and approached one of the empty corners. He had the next banner up before Serana found the sense to stop staring and finish organizing the programs.

They worked fast, in utter and complete silence—just the way she liked it. Mirabelle and the others preferred to gossip and meander. Between her and Logan, there was no need for fake cordiality or politeness, just swift efficiency. By the time he finished hanging the banners, she was already in the middle of doing the same task for the fifth time.

"Anything else?" A rush of warm breath ruffled her hair, sending her heart into overdrive as she turned to face the man behind her. For the first time, she viewed him in full and nearly choked once she spied a bulge at the front of his jeans—two bulges, one of the biological variety and the other…

She snuck another glance and felt her pulse pick up. *No way.* That couldn't be what it looked like. Right?

"Do you need help with anything else?" Logan repeated, drawing her attention back to his face.

"N-no."

To her surprise, they had finished it all. Even the rest of the banners hung neatly over the walls in perfect symmetry. In fact…she could have sworn that he must have *rehung* the banners she'd done on her own as well.

Or, she was being paranoid? Considering what he had in his pocket, she had every right to be.

"Thanks," she said, eyeing one of the tables behind him instead of his face. "You didn't have to help me."

"But I did," Logan replied, with a deep, unsettling chuckle. "So, how are you going to thank me?"

"Asshole." Suddenly, Serana wasn't so grateful. "You know what I should do? Call the police. Is this your idea of retaliation for what happened earlier? Bringing a knife here?"

She nodded to the object boldly sticking out of his pants pocket. It hadn't been a trick of the light—the bastard had an actual weapon.

"Were you planning on cornering me here alone?" Her voice trembled, revealing just how seriously she was considering that scenario.

He smiled, but she had to admit that it wasn't the sadistic grin of a man who intended to harm her. "No." He brushed his palm over the blade as if he'd forgotten it were there in the first place. "I came here to talk to you."

His tone was level enough. She couldn't tell if the statement was a harmless fact or a dangerous threat.

"How did you even know I was here? Mirabelle?"

He shrugged as his eyes glittered mischievously. "Let's just say, I have my methods."

Serana flinched. That sounded creepier than reassuring.

"Stalking?"

His face fell as if he took the possibility as a personal insult. "You drew my blood. Of course, I could find you—" He broke off abruptly, but Serana's mind was already reeling from the strange choice of phrasing.

"Did you put a hit out on me or something?" Deep down, she knew she was being irrational. As if a true hardened criminal could ever be found in Meyweather.

Though, Logan raised an eyebrow rather than deny the charge outright.

Which confused her even more. "Did you just get out of prison or something? It isn't every man who feels the need to walk around with a weapon."

He chuckled, but his eyes were downcast. Almost as if… She'd hit the nail right over the head.

"Let's just say, I'm not from around here."

"Oregon, was it?" she sniped, crossing her arms. "Don't tell me you expect anyone to buy that bullshit story." The fact that Mirabelle seemed to was beside the point. "Where are you really from?"

"Somewhere far from here," he replied. "Not Oregon."

Which made her first guess far more likely.

"A prison?"

He chuckled, but his eyes were narrowed in a way that made her suspect she'd caught him off guard. Which thrilled her for some reason. She wanted to do so again.

"Somewhere far from here," he repeated. "Some may refer to it as a prison, though who am I to judge?"

Did she believe him? Kind of. Something in his tone made her belly quiver. A low, hoarse note as if he didn't want to respond at all. But he had.

And she was too damn curious for her own good. "What did you do? Assault someone? Sell drugs?"

He eyed her for so long she was sure he wouldn't answer. Then, he inclined his head, his expression unreadable. "And if I said I killed someone?"

Her throat went dry. "Then I'd say that you couldn't be related to Mirabelle Harris."

Serana once saw the woman cry after accidentally squishing a spider. No one with those genes could actually be dangerous.

Right?

"But if you did," she added hastily. "Why?"

He blinked as if caught off guard by such a direct question. "The point is, I'm not there anymore," he said dismissively. Then he advanced a step toward her. "I'm here. With you."

Serana didn't move a muscle, sensing that to retreat would be to feed whatever sick kick he got by finding her alone in the first place. "And why is that? Don't tell me that you can't find someone else to play with."

"You're different," he said softly. "I'm not sure if that's a good thing."

"Different, how?" she demanded. A part of her expected him to croon some stupid, cliché line about how sexy she was. How beautiful. How…

"You're feisty," he said, but his furrowed brows betrayed that he didn't consider the term a compliment. "Like you belong in Hell rather than out here."

Well then. He earned points for creativity, at least. Regardless, she went cold, horrified by the possibility that he knew more of her past than she'd like him to. Had Mirabelle run her mouth?

Rather than give her fear away, she squared her chin.

"I don't think a pretty boy like you would last a second in Hell," she tossed back. Figuratively at least, she knew a thing or two about fire and brimstone. "My guess is you're an addict who got off on possession charges, but like to pretend you're some big-time criminal. I suggest you ride out your probation, go to rehab, and learn some manners. Might I suggest Daily Peace? We're always open to new members."

Though if he did manage to do such a thing, she'd reject his application outright.

Logan laughed, but the sound was softer than she would have expected. "That's the second time I've had that offer today, but I'm no addict. As far as my incarceration in Hell goes, you got your timeframe wrong, by the way. A second in Hell? Oh no. Try twenty-six years."

Ah. He'd sounded way too serious, and Serana couldn't help herself—she imagined what he might have been through to characterize his life in such harsh terms.

An absentee father? Or something worse…

A parent as cruel as the devil himself? A real addiction that nearly ruined his life? Unfortunately, she wasn't in the mood to commiserate with a complete stranger over shitty upbringings.

"Well, I don't give a damn where you're from," she snapped. "Now, get out of my way."

She attempted to shove by him, but he moved *faster*, pinning her against the banquet table.

"I don't usually accept insults as a form of payment, either," he murmured, eyeing her bottom lip. "But this time, I'll make an exception. To answer your question, I could find another woman to play with, but something tells me she won't hit back half as hard as you will. I prefer the challenge."

Shit. Her heart thudded ominously against the wall of her chest while she grappled with a building fear. As previously mentioned, this guy was related to *Mirabelle*—how badass could he be?

Plenty, a part of her whispered. She'd doubted his wholesome rancher from the west story the second she'd heard it. There was nothing at all wholesome about the thick cords of muscle coiled beneath his skin. Still...he really wouldn't stoop to assaulting her against a metal folding table in a community rec room.

Would he?

"Back off," she snapped, hating the slight tremor in her voice. "I have pepper spray in my purse and I'm not afraid to use it."

Though she had yet to deploy it on another person. There was a first time for everything.

"I will," Logan said. Instead, he leaned in. Close enough for the heat of his breath to baste her throat. "Just tell me one thing—answer me one question, as payment for my helping you."

Serana gave him the dirtiest look she could manage. Even so, the offer was tempting enough to risk humoring him for a second longer. "What?"

Suddenly, his mouth formed a stern line. "Do you work overtime to push people away? Or do you just like being alone?"

"The second one," she replied through gritted teeth.

The answer didn't seem to satisfy him, though. He merely inclined his head with a knowing glance that itched at her pride. "No, I think you like being in *control*," he said. "You don't like losing it, do you? Afraid it might kill you to let your hair down once in a while? You can't even let yourself accept a compliment from a stranger without getting defensive."

Ouch. She hadn't expected that. A creepy jab at her sexuality, maybe? Some more back-handed innuendo?

Not that.

"And do *you* work overtime to soothe your ego?" she bit back. "Did I hurt your feelings that badly just by refusing to drool at the sight of you? Newsflash, Logan—you aren't the center of the universe, and not everyone wants to fuck you."

She was bluffing—kind of—a man like him wouldn't give a damn whether she was interested in him or not. But then his eyes widened, alluding to the unthinkable.

She'd hit the bullseye.

"At least I have the balls to answer that question," Logan replied. His lips formed a surprisingly thoughtful frown. Perhaps he had brains in addition to brawn? "*Yes.* You turned me down. I want to know why, because *newsflash*—not many women do. Unless you aren't into men."

Because he was sex on legs and knew as much—and he possessed a fragile ego, to boot. It was only natural that someone so visually perfect would have a few character flaws to compensate. His entire demeanor screamed just how much her rejection bothered him. His jaw was clenched, his eyes a simmering green. Almost as if he truly had never been turned down before.

By anyone.

"Well, Logan, you're not my type," Serana quipped, "and after the way you've been acting, I think that's a good thing. And no, I'm not a lesbian, but I don't have a fetish for talking dicks. Now get the hell out of my way—" She shifted to evade him, but he effortlessly blocked her in from another angle.

Consequently, he was closer than ever. "Wait," he demanded. His eyes no longer simmered with amusement. They were hard, revealing flits of gold mingled amongst all that green.

"It's your turn. Answer the question, sweetheart. Or does it scare you to give up the reins even for a second? Trust me, it can be fun to let someone else take charge for a change, or even for a night, all fun, no strings attached. I may not be the center of the universe, but believe me, I don't want to be. People who don't want to fuck me, tend to prefer *killing* me, so where do you stand?"

His inflection dipped toward a dangerous baritone. No longer was this a game. Unfortunately for him, Serana wasn't in the mood to play.

"Go screw yourself," she hissed, wishing for another box cutter to slice the bastard with. Her nails would do nicely, though, and with a growl of annoyance, she lashed out.

Logan caught her wrist mid-air—but his grip wasn't painful or restraining. His eyes widened, almost as if he *wanted* her to hit him.

More than anything in the world.

Wrenching her hand away, she flinched back.

"I have no problem getting myself off," he responded to her taunt, his eyes glued to her trembling hands. "But I'd rather fuck *you* tonight instead."

Her mouth dropped open. *The motherfucking bastard said what*—before she'd fully recovered from the shock, he brought his face inches from hers.

"I can start with a kiss, though," he murmured. "Or will that upset your delicate sensibilities?"

Asshole. To say he didn't give her a choice would be a lie. He moved slowly and withdrew his hands to provide her with an open exit. She had a second, maybe two, to easily dodge his incoming mouth with room to spare.

But she didn't.

He seemed as surprised as she was when his mouth finally made contact. His lips were moist, unbelievably soft, and when he probed her with his tongue...

For a moment, she forgot where she was. *Who* she was— and he took advantage of her shock to shove his tongue down her throat.

Mayday! Caught off guard, Serana reacted the only way she knew how—she bit down like a sprung bear trap. She expected him to roar with pain and rear back. Maybe even hit her.

What she did not expect was for him to…growl. An actual *growl* that rippled from his throat like thunder and traveled down her spine. Not a sound of anger or pain, but one of those "fuck yeah" rumbles that her family's dog used to make whenever his belly was rubbed in just the right spot.

There was no other explanation. She'd bitten him…and the bastard *liked* it.

She released his tongue in confusion, and he lunged, shoving her against the table. Expertly, he managed to deepen the kiss, coaxing her mouth into submission with only a few gentle strokes. Then *pain*. He'd nipped at her lower lip as if in punishment for hurting him first. *Whoa.* The sensation was like nothing she'd ever…

Electric. Explosive. Terrifying.

She told herself that she *had* to grab him—it was either that or be crushed between his weight and the table. She had to let him muscle in closer.

But she didn't have to kiss him back. At some point, her hands curled over his shoulders, gripping the startling hardness. Was he all muscle? At the prospect, her fingers trembled, tightening their grip.

Another low sound rippled from his chest in response. Almost a purr… As if the sensation of her nails nicking his flesh was the hottest fucking thing in the world.

And he was pretty aroused already. The bulge brushing against her stomach wasn't one of his fists—both of which were inching dangerously close to her butt, or the handle of the blade sticking out of his front pocket. A tingle of fear darted down her spine as the weapon in question prodded her hip. It was real.

Though, he didn't seem inclined to use it on her at the moment. She instinctively guessed where his hands would slide next, and sure enough, they crept downward to cup her ass.

Focus girl! Panicked, she struggled to recall the self-defense class she'd taken back in college. What had the sensei said? Something about using every trick in the book to get back at a bastard who had you pinned.

No pain, no gain.

Squeezing her eyes shut, Serana called upon that old advice and jerked forward, ramming her head into his. The moment he fell back, she stumbled away—but not without grabbing that knife from his pocket first.

"Stay back," she rasped, waving that blade wildly. It was heavy. She felt as if she were a child playing with a toy, but she didn't want to drop it any time soon. "How is this for unpredictable? What's wrong? You don't like being out of *control* for once?"

Logan didn't seem intimidated in the least. In a heartbeat, he pivoted to stand behind her. "Easy, sweetheart." She felt his lips against her ear as he spoke. His mocking tone and a sexy chuckle made her breath catch. "Give me my knife back. This is me asking nicely."

"You want your *knife*?" she asked, surprised at how gritty her voice was.

The answer Logan grunted against her shoulder could have been, "Hell yes!"

"Well—" Her grip tightened over the handle. "Then, take it!"

She jabbed the butt of the handle in his direction, but Logan caught her by the wrist before she could make contact. Undeterred, she flexed her knees, utilizing her entire body to push him off.

As soon as she felt the solid muscle of his thighs against her back, she knew she was in trouble. Even before she heard the sound ripping from him.

It wasn't human—but something primal, guttural, deep.

Without warning, he shoved her onto the banquet table and flipped her over. His burning emerald gaze held her captive as he palmed the table on either side of her.

When his fingers reached down to cup her heatedly through the fabric of her pants, Serana knew she was in deep, *deep* shit.

Logan couldn't remember the last time he'd been so turned on. Wait, scratch that. He couldn't remember being so *accidentally* turned on.

The scary thing was that Serana Blake had no idea what she was doing to him. Every scratch drove him insane, and every wicked scrape of her teeth pushed him beyond his limits. In a matter of time, he would become too excited prematurely—something he hadn't experienced since his early teens.

Damn…

Groaning, he eyed the woman beneath him and tried to remember that she wasn't his type. Though hell, why wasn't she? Her body appealed to him well enough—particularly the pair of breasts heaving against the fabric of her sweater.

Apparently, she wasn't flat-chested after all. His mouth watered as he ached to rip off the bothersome fabric and see for himself…

One minor detail held him back. *She doesn't want you,* a part of him hissed. *She wants you to fuck off, remember?*

Right. But it was so hard to think clearly with the front of his jeans throbbing. Especially after she'd tried to hit him there. And, good God, the feel of being crushed against the heat of her body had been so…

Logan figured the only part of his admonishment to register in his brain was "fuck." Which, his body seemed more than ready to do. Still, he inhaled deeply and pulled back. *Slow down.*

His growing attraction aside, Serana didn't want him, and he didn't force the unwilling.

Ever.

"I'm sorry." He stood back, shaking his head to clear it. "I'm sorry. I'll go." He turned to leave, but her expression made him freeze.

She didn't look relieved, or even angry. Her lips were parted, but a stream of insults didn't spill from them next. Just one breathless word, "Wait…"

God help him, he *did*, feeling every muscle in his body twitch with restraint. Perhaps he'd read her wrong? Control wasn't her thing in the slightest. No. She *liked* living on the edge…

Though, she said nothing to confirm that hope. She didn't move, either. Her eyes were so wide that for a moment, he thought he might be swallowed up by silver. *Mayday*, a part of him warned. From experience, he knew he had about five seconds to turn away before he could do something he'd regret.

One…two…

Five—he held her gaze stubbornly, and a growl caught in his throat, as he imagined those gray eyes widening in ecstasy.

Oh yes. He was in trouble. Even more so when he reached down to cup that tiny sliver of fabric shielding the flesh between her thighs, and her legs parted of their own accord.

He almost wished she'd attack him again. Swear, kick, punch—*anything*.

Anything but gasp, bite her lip, and…whimper.

In the wake of that little sound, every thought left his mind. Groaning, he leaned over her again, finding the clasp of her slacks.

"I don't want to hurt you, Serana," he insisted as she sucked in a breath. "You want me to stop, I'll stop."

Without ever breaking eye contact, he slowly undid the metal fastenings and toyed with the zipper just long enough to feel her shudder, before pulling it down, down, down…

I'm an ass, was all he thought before ogling the silky fabric revealed through the open fly of her pants. *Black, lacy panties,* he realized with a grunt that caught in his throat. Though he knew without asking that she hadn't worn them in anticipation of another man.

The way she arched against his hand made him suspect it had been a long while since she'd been touched.

Though he wouldn't mind being her rebound fuck. He touched her again, sliding his finger deep within the gulf he could feel lying in wait beneath the slick fabric. This time... she shuddered, her eyelids fluttering.

Logan hissed, clenching his teeth. The pleasure roiling through his abdomen came as a shock. Sex with him had always been an *everyman for himself* type of deal—he had never been into foreplay.

But with Serana...

He had as much fun watching his finger torment her through the fabric of her panties, as he did buried inside most women.

Strange.

He blamed her—no one had ever reacted to him like this. Hungrily, but selfishly. Her body's reaction was undeniable —it wanted more—and she seemed to hate that fact. She bit her lip harder, as her throat jerked around a swallow.

He tensed again, expecting her to curse him to Hell and back.

Instead, her thighs twitched in a silent invitation he didn't dare second-guess.

This time, when he stroked her, he watched the heat flood her face. Watched her eyes dart down to his hand and stay there. Watched *her* watch as his fingers rocked against her. Over and over and *over*.

Damn, it wasn't enough. He wanted to feel her part beneath his fingers. Wanted to drink in her pleasured moans. Hear her pant his name.

Only then, with her right on the edge, would he take her hard and fast until she shattered—

"Serana?"

The distant voice buzzed at the edge of his consciousness, but he couldn't remember why those lilting tones were important. Mattered.

It wasn't until he heard the metal door being tried from the outside that he finally jolted to awareness. *Shit!*

"Serana?" The knocking came from the outer doors leading directly to the parking lot. The voice, however, was chillingly familiar. Mirabelle. "Serana?" she called. "Are you still here?"

"Mirabelle…" He barely recognized Serana's voice. It was so faint and broken he instantly felt guilty—which was so damn weird.

Almost as weird as the prospect of his half-sister finding him in the process of seducing one of her coworkers.

Snapping to his senses, he bolted upright and helped Serana up.

She looked dazed, as if she were in the middle of a dream, and Logan felt the need to steady her with his hand as she fumbled to close her pants.

"Oh, God—" like saucers, her eyes darted to those shuddering doors. "Mirabelle. She can't see me like this."

Logan seconded that. Luckily, after all his sexual exploits over the years, he was used to composing himself in the blink of an eye. Already, he had adjusted his T-shirt to cover the worst of the bulge threatening to burst through his zipper. The woman beside him, on the other hand, still had her fly open.

Something unfamiliar unraveled in his chest as he wrenched her zipper back into position.

He couldn't stop his fingers from lingering there, though. From wishing more than anything he could remove all her clothing and finish what they'd started.

He was a horn-dog, sure—but this…

The lust charging through him was unlike anything he'd ever felt.

Ever.

Maybe because she still hated his guts.

"Serana?" Mirabelle continued her frantic knocking, and Serana flinched.

"S-shit." She lunged for the table and grabbed something he couldn't see until it was too late—his *knife*. Her shaking fingers gripped the handle, and she swiped it at him, forcing Logan on his heels.

"Get the fuck away from me!"

Well, so much for their mutual attraction. Logan tried to ignore the disappointment that ripped through his chest as he rushed to the doors before Mirabelle knocked them down.

"Fix your hair," he called over his shoulder. Then, he undid the lock and stood back as his "cousin" stumbled inside.

"Logan?" He tried not to flinch as Mirabelle's blue eyes took him in. She looked instantly skeptical, as if he were as out of place in this room as an elephant in a china store. He followed her gaze over to Serana, who had fully recovered, seeming more frigid than ever. Almost. She had one arm behind her back, hiding his knife from view.

"Is everything alright?" Mirabelle asked. "We don't usually keep that door locked."

"Everything's fine," Logan lied. He slid in front of her, pulling her slender body in for an impromptu hug—distracting her long enough for Serana to shove his blade beneath a stack of pamphlets before she saw it.

"Serana?" Mirabelle turned to the woman in question. "Are you alright?"

Serana certainly didn't seem alright, but she nodded anyway, cheeks flaming. "I'm fine…but," her voice took on a hard edge. "What are *you* doing here?"

Mirabelle flashed a sheepish smile. "I felt so bad about leaving earlier. I came back to see if you needed any help."

Serana looked confused. As if she wasn't used to having someone admit that they were wrong—at least not to her face. That gratitude lasted all of two seconds though, before an icy expression replaced it.

"Thanks, but no thanks. I managed to get everything done without you."

Mirabelle's eyebrows shot up and a faint pink colored her cheeks. "I'm sorry, Serana," she said softly. "I shouldn't have left."

"Well. There's nothing left to do, and I'm really tired, so…"

"Of course." Mirabelle swallowed and fidgeted with the hem of her yellow coat. "You're right. We have a busy day tomorrow. I'll just help you close up—"

"No!" Serana exclaimed, though Logan figured her refusal had more to do with his knife being partially hidden behind a stack of pamphlets than genuine animosity.

"Come on, Mirabelle," he said, stepping forward. "I'll walk you home."

"Well, okay." She glanced back at Serana, unease showing in her blue eyes. "I'll see you tomorrow?"

Serana sighed. "Yes. Eight o'clock sharp."

With that, Logan rushed to lead Mirabelle from the rec center, but not before sparing one last glance at the woman who'd managed to set him on fire without even trying.

Next time, he thought, flicking his gaze up over that slender body. He did a double take though, as his gaze fell over hers. Those gray eyes stared dead into his own, and it was all he could do to breathe.

In the end, Mirabelle was the one to steer *him* through the double doors. As it turned out, she'd come by car and didn't need an escort either. Alone, he headed toward the pub instead. He'd probably spend the rest of the night camped out by the bar, downing drink until he couldn't *think,* let alone recall this little tryst.

Bullshit.

He doubted even a bad hangover would erase the sight of her from his mind. Because…for a brief, brief moment so quick he was sure that he imagined it, it looked like she wanted him to stay.

And he would have been more than willing to. Though he'd be damned if he knew why.

SIX

*F*uck *Mirabelle*, Serana thought coldly.

No…wait, on second thought fuck Logan *and* Mirabelle. No, wait, she didn't want to fuck Logan at all. *Or* Mirabelle…

"Fuck!" Exhausted, Serana dropped to her knees and rested her forehead on the nearest table, hoping the cold surface would help snap her out of it.

What the hell was she doing?

What the hell had she *done*?

Not the right, responsible thing—such as marching over to her purse, withdrawing her cell phone, and punching in the number to 911 to report a sexual assault.

Logan was clearly a deviant who needed to be locked up before he harassed someone else. *But,* she thought, before she could stop herself, *is it really sexual assault if you love every minute of it? Not to mention, didn't exactly ask him to stop...*

Her mouth dropped open in horror at the realization. She hadn't *enjoyed* what Logan did to her. She hadn't...

But she *had* let him unzip her pants. She had let him kiss her, and hadn't exactly fought back when he tried to go farther than that.

"God..."

Children played here after school.

The local church used this same table for their annual bake sale in the spring, and she had all but had sex, right on top of it.

With a guy who seemed ripped from a Greek epic with the attitude of a frat boy. It didn't matter that he was related to Mirabelle, the town sweetheart. The bastard needed to leave, *tonight.*

Yes, Serana decided to make his expulsion from Meyweather her personal mission—right after she took a hot shower to erase the feel of him off her. Though, she suspected it would take a lot more than a loofah and soap.

The bastard is a menace, she tried to tell herself. An irresistible, teasing menace who'd made her feel things she hadn't...

Ever.

Get over it. Her first, and coincidentally her only, boyfriend, Mark, had said all the things Logan had.

He promised to love her forever and ever, as he laid her out in the back of his father's pickup truck. From what little she could remember of the sex, it hadn't lasted much longer than the few seconds it took to close her eyes and count to ten.

Almost as long as their entire "relationship" had lasted.

The next week Mark had come to school with none other than Kathy Wilson, a Mirabelle 1.0, who was so beautiful and kind that even Serana felt guilty for hating her. That day, she realized the cold, hard truth as if it had been driven in with a serrated blade the size of a prom corsage—she would always be the backup.

The plan B.

Mark Kell had really wanted Kathy Wilson, and Serana had been nothing more than just a stepping-stone in his way. He didn't even have the decency to break up with her in person—he seemed to expect her to know that it was over.

Even after all this time, it still stung, and no hot-ass loser in skin-tight jeans would be enough to make her open herself up for more pain.

No siree.

Gritting her teeth, she slammed her hand down, hoping the pain would knock some sense back into her. But she got way more than she bargained for.

"Ow!" Hissing, she drew her hand back, watching in shock as a drop of her blood dripped onto a handful of the clinic fundraiser programs. It wasn't until she pushed them aside with her good hand that she saw the blade hiding underneath.

Damn it. She'd almost forgotten stealing it from Logan.

It wasn't your average kitchen knife—that was for damn sure. Her father had been a hunter, and this finely-honed blade with a slight curve looked nothing like a hunting blade.

The surface was etched with designs. Ebony and indigo curls started off silver on the hilt but darkened once they hit the metal. Expensive metal if the shine was anything to go by. Silver, maybe? Or even platinum.

Definitely, a gang weapon.

In fact, Serana had a feeling that if she dropped this little baby off at the police station, a quick run through the system would pick up multiple hits, related to street brawls and drug violence.

Oddly enough, she wasn't so inclined. Yet. She picked it up with her uninjured hand and tested its weight. It was much lighter than she expected, not at all heavy. She slipped it into her pocket on impulse, the way Logan had done.

"Holy..." She jumped as she tossed the thing onto the table as if it were on fire.

It *burned.*

She half expected the pamphlets beneath it to melt. But they didn't. Taking a few napkins from a nearby table, she tentatively picked up the blade again, trying not to touch the hilt. Then, she dropped it into her purse.

She felt a tinge of guilt as she swung the bag over her arm, but stubborn pride replaced it. Let the bastard beg for it back—not that she would think of him. To aid in said amnesia, she would need a shower tonight, alright. A cold one. *Frigid,* she insisted as her eyes caught sight of the rumpled banquet table.

It didn't take long to fix the mess. Clutching the napkins in her bleeding palm, she picked out the few blood-smeared pamphlets and threw them in the trash. Then, she shoved the table back on center and left before she lost her nerve and camped out on the clinic floor instead.

She'd done it before. Some nights *anything* was better than going back to her father's empty old house. A night curled up on the ratty armchair in her office did wonders compared to that queen-sized mattress anyway.

One fact was enough to make her sigh and head out into the cold night.

The office didn't have a shower.

SEVEN

Logan was sure the moment he returned to Marcus' bar, he would collapse onto a stool and go through bottles of the man's best stuff like a kid in a candy store.

He had instead taken the detour to the apartment and hopped straight into the shower, turning the water on blast to the coldest temperature possible.

In the midst of the rush, he stood fully clothed.

Good God…Serana Blake was going to be the death of him. Already he could feel himself aching for her, just thinking of her name, despite the frigid water pelting his back.

It wasn't like he wanted to marry the woman or anything. He wanted…

To prove her wrong. Hell, perhaps he sought the very thing he'd taunted her with—for her to lose control. To feel her breath hot and heavy on his neck as she tore at his clothing with the same desperation that he tore at hers. He wanted her panting his name as he took her to the edge.

And he had no damn idea *why*.

It might have been the simple fact that she had called him out. He couldn't handle rejection. Shaels thrived on intimacy, but fear of commitment wasn't where his insecurities lay. Oh, hell no. As long as he was on top of a woman, she couldn't put a knife in his back.

Though who was a mortal to send him on a path of reviewing his personal emotional turmoil?

"Damn her!" He slammed his fist into the wall of the shower, shattering a tile.

Great. Just one more thing he'd owe Marcus for—not that the man seemed to be keeping tabs.

Wasn't that what brothers were for? He had no damn idea. Being incarcerated hadn't given him much time to get used to the concept of brotherhood. However, Marcus had treated him better than most.

Though that didn't say much. Marcus had yet to threaten him, at least. He'd even paid his passage into the mortal realm, which put him on the minuscule list of people Logan could recall ever helping him out without demanding something in return. He might have doubted they were related at all, until he remembered their mother was an evil slut who'd collected part-daemon children for shits and giggles.

It wasn't just the two of them. There was another—a brother, *Jace*, who'd been so fucked up by their shattered upbringing that he hadn't even wanted to show up to their initial cheery family reunion. And there was Mirabelle, his kind, thoughtful "cousin."

Family. A few years ago, he would have never thought that the word could apply to him. That he could have people out there he could actually *care* about, other than to just fuck or use when the need arose.

Maybe, someone like Serana Blake needed family? Again, he found himself thinking about her, ignoring the strain that it caused to the front of his jeans.

Regardless, she was a welcome distraction from the epic mess his life had become. His knowledge of her history was limited, but from what he could gather, her life hadn't been easy either. Sure, her folks had money—tons, if the number of signs around town bearing the name *Blake* were anything to go by. But money didn't exactly buy happiness, a truth Logan had learned firsthand.

A poor little rich girl with massive daddy issues who took out her problems on everyone was just one of a million stories.

But no... That wasn't it.

Logan knew hatred. He knew rage. He knew what it was like to want to shake a fist at the world and loathe everyone and everything with a pulse just because you *could.*

Serana was different. Instead of burning with rage, she seemed frozen—as if somehow, deep inside, she'd flipped a switch off to all emotion. Smothered it.

Why?

He chewed on his lip as he pondered the answer. Fear?

Bingo, he thought, smiling coldly as icy water dripped off his skin to circle the drain. She was afraid. Serana, who'd stabbed him for an insult, was afraid of anyone getting too close.

Too bad that person wasn't him. Ignoring the delicious challenge of breaking her walls down, he just wasn't into commitment.

He almost regretted that—he hadn't been lying when he'd claimed to be a perfectionist. He hated leaving things half undone, and when he fucked Serana it would have been nice to experience all she was, just once.

Oh, because he *would* fuck her. Her fate was sealed the moment she stole his blade and attacked him with it. As if Krall, would ever harm him wielded by a mortal's clumsy hand.

Speaking of Krall…

He reached into his pocket for the blade, aiming to toss it onto the bathroom rug to protect its sheath—but it wasn't there.

"What the hell?"

An image of the rec room filled his head, paired with the sight of Serana shoving his blade under a pile of pamphlets…

"Shit!"

Krall, his blade—the only thing in the world capable of killing him, let alone neutralizing the harbinger of doom—was lying unguarded in the middle of a mortal community center.

Logan burst into the hallway dripping wet and took the stairs two at a time. He was halfway to the door when Marcus' voice stopped him dead.

"The cold shower didn't work, I take it?"

"Err…fuck!" It was the only coherent sound Logan could make before he barged onto the street.

If Krall had fallen into the wrong hands, out there, loose for the picking, he figured stealth wasn't an option.

At full speed, it took him all of ten seconds to reach the rec center. Serana and Mirabelle weren't in view, and neither was anyone who might have been able to let him inside. Therefore, he had no choice but to barge in through a side door amid a screeching alarm.

"Logan, have you lost your fucking mind?"

For the first time, he noticed that Marcus was hot on his heels. Unconcerned, he tore through the banquet table while Marcus hustled off to silence the alarm.

With his fist.

It took all of two seconds, after swiping all the programs onto the floor, to realize that his blade wasn't there.

"Holy…" He had to lean over the table as the horror of his loss washed over him.

Without Krall by his side—close—any daemon with a nose to smell would be able to sense it. Find it. He didn't know all the specifics, but he still remembered the chilling words his mother had issued the very day she first presented him with the blade—*keep it on you always.* As he'd gotten older, he'd begun to fill in the blanks of what she'd left unsaid. Daemonic weapons were rare, tethered to the soul of their owner. Without Krall…

He was vulnerable in a way he'd never been—not to mention that he'd have a one-way ticket straight back to daemon prison, unable to fulfill his bargain.

The sound of approaching footsteps was the only thing that held him back from releasing another string of curses.

"What's wrong?"

"It's not here. Krall. I must have left it somewhere." He couldn't even look at Marcus.

"Damn," was all he said, and Logan was surprisingly grateful for that. "Do you think someone took it? It couldn't be a daemon—they would have torn the place apart."

Which *he* had done all on his own.

Still, as many years as he'd had the blade, no one had been able to take it off him. At least not until… "*Serana.*"

His eyes narrowed, even as his cock twitched at the sound of her name. She had his blade. Holy fuck. When he got his hands on her…

Marcus cleared his throat. "What do you mean Serana?"

Logan tried to ignore the suspicious edge to his tone. The fact that he'd disobeyed what seemed to be a direct order to stay away from the woman was beside the point. Serana had Krall, and by taking his blade, the mortal woman had no idea what on earth she'd done.

No fucking clue.

Oh, but he would enlighten her, alright.

"You need to get it back," Marcus said, his voice deliberately calm, but Logan knew that he would pay later. "*Soon*, preferably."

"Now," Logan insisted, gritting his teeth as he imagined all the ways he'd get Krall back from Serana—none of them very nice. One scenario even involved whips and chains and veered into surprisingly sexy territory that had nothing to do with revenge.

"Don't even think about it. You aren't going anywhere near her," Marcus replied.

Logan drew a fist and punched the table, compounding the damage he had already done. "Why not?"

"Mirabelle."

Ah. He let his hand fall as he followed Marcus' line of logic. His so-called cousin wouldn't like it if he barged into her friend's house to steal back a powerful, enchanted daemon blade. Or if he stabbed said friend in the process.

And then stabbed *her*.

"After today, I think we're in agreement," Marcus finished for him. "The less she knows, the better. That means keeping a low profile. No breaking into mortal homes. No chaos and bloodshed. You handle this properly."

Logan grunted in understanding. Though he despised the saying "ignorance is bliss," in Mirabelle's case, he was willing to make an exception. There were some things that no one should have to live with.

"You can get it back tomorrow," Marcus continued. "It's still in town, and not stolen by an errant daemon, so it should be okay to go at this with some tact. You'll still need to be careful. While I doubt any daemons will be able to sense Krall's aura out here, this far in the mortal realm, I'd rather not take the risk. Mortals aren't very withstanding against daemon attacks."

"I know." Logan flinched even at the thought of Serana coming into harm's way.

Still…

"Look." Marcus snatched one of the programs proclaiming a charity event the next day. "Meet her here. It's public, open spaces, lots of people."

Logan didn't answer right away. When he finally looked over, he found his brother staring pensively at his side, where his own blade was strapped beneath his shirt in a similar leather sheath.

"It's your life," the man said softly. "But try to remember that some of us might care enough to fight to the death should you lose it."

When they hustled out of the rec center, Logan knew in his gut that, whether he wanted him to or not, Marcus would always have his back.

Meanwhile, Logan had already sold him out.

EIGHT

Serana dreamt of fire. A *blade* made of fire, to be exact, stabbing into her thigh. She could feel it—the heat and metal and a sharp burst of pain that made her instinctively bite down so hard on her tongue she tasted blood.

But she didn't wake up. She couldn't wake up.

Because, while the blade was in her hand, she didn't *want* to. Wrapped between her fingers, the handle felt…perfect. Right, like a part of herself she hadn't even been aware of until then.

Slowly, she stroked her thumb along the edge, and the heat prickling her skin intensified—so much so she bit her lip to keep from crying out.

Shaking from head to toe, she steeled herself to look down, expecting to see her side smeared with blood and the metal of the knife sinking deep. All she saw instead was…gold.

Golden hair that flexed beneath her fingers instead of a hilt, while a tongue teased her instead of a blade.

At the sight, the heat only intensified, building into a smoldering, heart-stopping inferno that had her gasping for air.

Logan. His name made her body ripple. Helpless, she gripped his scalp as his mouth inched closer to where she needed him the most.

Suddenly, he disappeared, and she was holding the blade again, this time brandished high into the air above her head.

Crawl. The word echoed through her skull with such an intensity she whimpered beneath the onslaught.

But no… It wasn't a word, but older sounding—more like, *Krall.* A name.

The blade had a name. And for some reason, it wanted her to know it…

Right before it plunged into her chest.

She woke up screaming. As her eyes opened, she bolted upright, shoving back the blankets which had become twisted into a cocoon around her.

She'd been sweating. Her entire body was drenched, gluing her nightshirt to her skin, even though the room itself felt frigid. Not only that, but her hand hurt. Instinctively, she'd woken up with it clutched against her chest, and even in the darkness, she could tell that the cut was a whole lot deeper than she'd initially thought.

Just as unsettling, the skin on the left side of her chest burned, right below her clavicle. Throbbed. On top of it all, her entire body just ached.

Though for various reasons.

Coffee, she decided, lurching to her feet. She needed caffeine, and lots of it, if she'd been dreaming about a total creep like Logan.

Her bare feet hit the carpet as she padded from her room and down the stairs in pitch darkness.

Her father had always kept the place brimming with light—lamps switched on even in the daytime. As a kid, she remembered wondering if he was afraid the slightest shadow might obscure one of his precious possessions.

But it wasn't until she reached adulthood that she realized the man feared the dark just like everyone else. He had hated the silence of it and tried to distract from the inevitable with the noise of large parties and chattering guests.

Wow, she realized, leaning heavily against the doorway to the kitchen as a sudden pain stabbed through her chest. *It's been a while since I've thought like that...*

Too long. Not long enough.

While some people loved to relish memories of their childhood, she hated venturing back to that cold, dead place in her soul where those old memories lay. She hated reliving them.

Hated knowing that nothing much had changed. After all those years as a child, dreaming of a perfect future, she'd failed by ending up just like *him*.

Alone.

Unwanted.

Hated.

That was poetic justice at its finest, but the memories did serve *one* useful purpose.

They kept her sharp. Kept her…smart. Whenever she felt tempted to crack. To fall apart. To let someone else in. She'd only have to remember the cold voice of her father whispering that she'd never be "good enough." Pretty enough. Sweet enough. Kind enough.

As masochistic as it seemed, the thoughts dispelled the pain, similar to honing her emotions on the edge of a grindstone to keep them sharp. Like a sword.

Or…a knife. She found herself turning on her heel, slipping through the foyer where her purse rested on an end table. Inside still rested Logan's blade.

Finger's shaking, she wrapped them around the hilt and pulled it out slowly, waiting for any flash of pain. It didn't burn, at least. Tentatively, she trailed a finger along the edge of the blade, marveling at just how sharp it was.

Yep. Logan definitely had to be a criminal gangbanger to possess a weapon like this.

Carefully, she cradled the blade in both hands and headed through the foyer and into her father's old study. Once she flipped on a light, she inspected the weapon in full. The blade was a type of metal with a shine unlike anything she'd ever seen—minus, a splotch of her blood.

Which was odd. She'd cut herself hours ago, but the crimson bead still looked fresh. In fact, when she swiped her finger over it, it easily spread, painting the metal.

Funny. It must have been cold enough inside the house to keep the blood from drying. She was shivering, now that the heat of the dream was gone. Her teeth even started to chatter as she reached under the desk for the gun safe her father kept there.

She didn't know why she hadn't sold these things yet. It freaked her out, having them in the house, though just the thought of going through his stuff at all gnawed at her like a bad stomachache. The feeling wasn't because of nostalgia, but fear…

She was afraid of the old, forgotten memories that had become trapped in the crevices of this place. Things she didn't want to remember. Feelings she'd long left behind as a little girl.

Even the sight of his pistols inside the gun safe made her jaw ache. She could still remember the first one he'd ever bought—a revolver, he called Betty, his favorite of them all.

He took to cleaning *Betty* often, usually when he was angry about something, sometimes right in front of her.

One pull on the trigger, Serana, he'd tell her while guiding a rag with polish carefully over the barrel. *And it's over.*

Some days, she wondered if that had been his way of warning her about what might come several years down the road.

One pill too many on her part, and a sole pull of the trigger on his.

Not going there, she thought firmly, shaking her head against the memory that threatened to break free. *Off-limits.*

Instead, she took off her nightshirt and wrapped Logan's blade in the thin material before placing it inside away from the other weapons.

She wasn't being sentimental or anything. It just didn't feel right to put that blade in among the others without protection.

Then, she flicked off the light and entered the kitchen to start a pot of coffee before heading back upstairs to get dressed. It was only later, while seated at the kitchen table, that she began to remember bits of her dream. Against her will, of course, but that little detail didn't really seem to matter as the image of Logan licking eagerly at her thigh almost made her spill hot coffee on her lap.

Holy…

Even in her dreams, the guy knew how to use his tongue. *Knew how not to quit,* she interjected angrily, hating the fact that tendrils of heat still curled in her belly at the thought of him.

But, he hadn't been the only one in her dream, she remembered after taking a steadying sip of pure black brew. The only *thing*.

She'd dreamed of his knife. *Which,* a part of her sighed, *is how you know you've got it bad—when you start dreaming about a guy's weapon.*

But, it wasn't just any weapon…

It had a name.

She knew it in her bones. Knew it in…her soul. Logan's knife had a name.

Krall.

A name that had come to her in her dreams.

A name she could still hear echoing in her skull.

Krall!

That's it, Serana, she scolded herself while taking another deep swig of coffee. *No more late nights for you.*

But the late nights didn't bother her. It was the loneliness that was the kicker.

NINE

A barrage of knocking on the front door, paired with a frantic voice calling her name, jolted Serana awake. Lurching to her feet, she tried to make sense of the incessant pounding.

Had someone died?

Was her house on fire?

Better yet, had the police descended upon her for possessing a blade that was probably wanted in connection to some grisly murder?

It was only when her eyes fell across the microwave that she caught sight of the time.

"Shit!" She scrambled out of the kitchen, pausing only to chuck her empty coffee mug in the sink and scrape her hair into a bun. Then, she hurtled down the hallway to the front door, wrenching it open just as Mirabelle had her fist raised to start another round of pounding.

"Serana!" the woman exclaimed. "Thank God. Do you know what time it is? When you didn't show up, I thought that…"

Serana gestured Mirabelle inside, all while trying to smooth her hair. "I overslept," she muttered by way of explanation.

Mirabelle didn't seem satisfied. "Are you…feeling okay?"

Serana frowned. Going off Mirabelle's expression, she could only imagine how shitty she must have looked. After wasting the early morning drinking black coffee, she'd finally fallen asleep at the kitchen table a little after dawn. All in all, she guessed that she'd gotten three hours of sleep, max.

"Fine," she lied, tucking a wayward curl behind her ear.

Mirabelle didn't look very convinced. She stood awkwardly in the foyer with her tan messenger bag clutched to her chest in a way that made Serana suspect that she was trying her hardest not to touch anything.

Though, that might have had to do more with the fact that she was in the infamous Blake house than politeness.

"You're never late," the woman added.

Serana winced. "I know. Wait here," she called, before ascending the staircase. "I'll just be a minute."

It took literally just that amount of time to stick a toothbrush in her mouth, scrape at her face with a washcloth and hunt for a pair of new clothes. A few moments later, she appeared in the living room wearing a blouse and slacks

—though her hasty ensemble couldn't compare to Mirabelle's, who looked like a vision of perfection in a blue sundress.

Without a word, Serana grabbed her purse from the hallway and led Mirabelle out into an overcast morning. They took the other woman's car to the community center, and it was only there in the parking lot that Mirabelle finally spoke.

"Serana…"

Her wary tone caught Serana's attention. Instantly she turned, surprised to find Mirabelle glancing down at her hands with anxious blue eyes. "Listen…I don't think you did it, but."

"But what?" Serana couldn't help the way her heart started to pound. How the back of her throat itched as she tried to consider what could have possibly gone wrong.

Had the caterers fallen through? Had a significant number of RSVPs canceled, leaving the budget to fill in the gap?

They were barely in the black with this event—and that was only if they managed to rake in every bit of the money they expected to raise. They couldn't afford the slightest setback.

Mirabelle sighed. "You should see for yourself."

Serana didn't like the sound of that. Not one damn bit. Fingers shaking, she undid the buckle of her seatbelt and followed Mirabelle through the back entrance.

The others were already there, huddled near the center of the room. It took Serana all of two seconds to realize why

Mirabelle—and everyone else for that matter—looked so grim.

The pamphlets, what was left of them anyway, were all scattered over the floor. Someone had tried to arrange them neatly into piles, but there wasn't much they could do because the banquet table had been bent in half.

For a brief moment, Serana was afraid she was having a heart attack. What else could explain the pain tearing through her chest as she took in the ruined programs that had cost them hundreds to print? The ringing in her ears intensified as she tried to imagine how they could possibly come up with the money to cover the damage to the table.

Let alone the damage to the double doors of the other side entrance, which had been sealed shut and cordoned off with yellow caution tape.

"What the…" She couldn't even find the strength to finish the question. Instead, she just squeezed her eyes shut, allowing the perfectionist, controlled Serana to take her place before she did something she'd regret.

Like break down and scream.

"Gather up all of the programs and put them on the dinner tables instead," she said after forcing out a heavy sigh. She opened her eyes to find Amanda and Sarah rushing to do just that.

"Robbie, find us another table," she added, turning to glance at him from the corner of her eye. "Rachel and Paul, find us a maintenance man to fix the damn door and get that tape off of it."

"That's just the thing," Mirabelle spoke up from beside her, twirling her fingers around the strap of her handbag. "The police say we can't have the event here tonight. This was an act of vandalism—there's an open investigation—"

Serana stopped listening as she tried to imagine where the hell she could fit a fundraiser full of over fifty guests on such short notice.

Breathing deeply, she swayed on her feet as all around she could feel Amanda, Sara, and the others watching her every move.

What the hell was she supposed to do?

"We could always postpone?" Sara pitched in from her crouched position on the floor. "Push it back until next week?"

Serana shook her head, suddenly too exhausted to explain that the food catering had been purchased at a discount only for tonight. It would cost them bundles to reschedule —not to mention the cost of reprinting programs.

And new banners…

They were stretched thin as it was.

"My cousin!" The soft exclamation came from Mirabelle, who suddenly flashed a smile that could have charmed the sun from out behind the clouds. "Marcus. He owns a bar.

Maybe if we scrape a bit of extra money together in the budget, we could—"

Serana was already moving to the door. She paused only to beckon Mirabelle with a wave of her hand before she took off, almost running, across the street and down the block she knew Mirabelle's cousin Marcus' bar to be.

It was called the Seralis, or something like that.

According to the scattered bits of gossip she'd picked up from around the office, it was known to be a nice place. Clean, with decent drink and good food.

Please, please, just owe Mirabelle a favor, she thought fervently as she pulled open the door of the pub and stepped inside.

Her only hope was that Logan wasn't around. If she faced him now, who knew what she might do?

Damn Marcus and his rules. If Logan had done things his way, he would have had Krall back by now. Instead, he leaned against the bar and twirled a flimsy kitchen knife between his fingers while counting the minutes down. Made of cheap metal, the blade was a poor substitute. The edge couldn't even cut through his palm—let alone Mirabelle's.

Surprisingly, his freedom wasn't the main concern weighing on his mind. Fuck the hunters. Without Krall, he felt…

Weak. Vulnerable. Exposed.

Much like the terrified child he'd spent the past twenty years trying to outgrow. Serana had quipped that he wouldn't last a second in "real" Hell. She'd partly been right—though his mother left him to fend for himself, she had given him one small, shred of protection—Krall. It was more than a blade, but his security blanket in a sense. One small reminder that he was no longer weak, at the whims of those stronger.

Can't steal it, he tried to tell himself. *Think of Mirabelle. Think of Mirabelle...*

She probably wouldn't like it if he barged into Serana Blake's house, took his knife back, and maybe stole a few kisses along the way. Though, what he really wanted to do to the woman was...

Way too naughty for words. Much like his fondness for an intimate object, the lingering lust for the mortal puzzled him. Oh well. He could solve both problems for good once he sought her out later tonight. Until then, Marcus had forbidden him from leaving the pub, though he didn't plan on playing bartender any time soon.

When the bell above the door chimed to herald a customer, he didn't glance up, hoping the mortal patrons took the hint and left. Instead, a tentative voice called out.

"Hello?"

Damn. His head whipped up as he recognized the soft tones instantly—*her* voice. Sure enough, there she stood, framed in the doorway like a vision of black.

Her hair was slicked back in another tight bun, but a wayward curl had slipped loose, framing her jawline. He stared. It was the only thing about her that hadn't been smoothed back or beaten into submission. Logan itched to stroke it with his finger. Better yet, undo the entire mess and discover how long her hair really was.

Yeah. He'd love to run his fingers through that...

"Hello?" she called again, craning her neck to peer through the doorway that led to the kitchen where Marcus was getting things ready for the lunch rush. She hadn't seen him yet. Good.

Logan slipped from around the counter and came up behind her, scouring her empty hands for any hint of his blade. "Change your mind about my offer?"

He sure hoped so. Hell, he could hardly think of anything else—her for one night, no strings attached. Even concern for Krall couldn't compete.

"You." A scowl shaped her features as she spun to face him —but to his surprise, she didn't try to stab him.

Yet.

"I need to see Marcus," she said tightly. "It's urgent."

"What's wrong?" He was surprised by how rough his voice sounded. Had someone harmed her?

"Someone vandalized the rec room of the community center last night." Logan could tell that she fought to keep her voice steady, but he still heard a slight tremor anyway.

And the sound struck something inside of him. "What?"

While he would never assume to be able to predict mortals, something like that seemed out of place in such a small town.

Serana nodded. "They destroyed a table, trashed a stack of pamphlets, and caused damage to the side doors."

Uh oh. Logan turned away from her, and racked his mind, trying to remember just what he had done in his search for Krall.

"Shit," he hissed. A few things *definitely* might have been smashed along the way.

"The police won't let us have the fundraiser there with it being an open investigation," Serana went on. "Without a venue…we're screwed. Our government funding has already been cut this year. We'd have to trim our outreach efforts, and cut back on free exams. Daily Peace might even be dissolved, and there are people in this town who rely on that program. God, this is a mess."

Her voice broke. Just a slight little tremor that made Logan bite back the urge to rush over to her and…

"You really care?" he asked without taking a step. "About something you had no control over?"

It was a foreign concept in his world. Daemons played by very different rules than humans, politely summed up as kill or be killed.

"Of course, I care," she snapped. "I took on the responsibility, and if anything falls through, it's on me."

Her conviction itched at him. How odd was it that a mortal could take on such responsibility without flinching, but when it came to protecting his own siblings, all it took was a blond bitch, some threats, and the prospect of prison to make him cave?

At least in this instance, he wasn't so helpless.

"Wait here." He headed for the kitchen before she could question.

There, Marcus stood near the stove, stirring something in a large metal pot. "You guzzle all my best alcohol yet?" he asked dryly.

"No," Logan admitted, leaning against the doorway. "There won't be time, because we're going to host the clinic fundraiser tonight."

For a few seconds, Marcus just kept stirring. Then, he turned to fix Logan with a stare that would have made anyone else quiver in their boots.

"Oh really?" he asked. "And why am I going to do that?"

"Because," Logan began confidently, "*I'm* the one who trashed the rec room last night, rendering it off-limits, and you were basically an accomplice."

He actually felt guilty about that. Then again, there was that old saying about nothing getting in the way between a man and his knife. Or was it something else?—whatever.

He shrugged and fixed Marcus with a grin he hoped passed as charming. "It's the least we can do for her."

Or, the least *Marcus* could do—Logan was still coming up with several different ways to make it up to Serana personally. And none of them involved public, open spaces, or soirees.

He wanted to get her alone, and make her open up more— about why she took his knife, her past. Everything.

"Where am I going to get money to cover the overhead for an entire night?" Marcus asked, still quiet. "Even if I did offer to host, who's going to help serve?"

Logan held up his hand, ticking off every suggestion as he thought of a solution. "I'll work here to pay it off, and I'll serve. This way, I can get close to her, and get Krall back without causing a scene. It's a win-win."

Marcus just watched him, eyes dark. "I can't pay enough overtime to cover something like this. I'm stretched thin as it is."

Logan patted his front pocket, and—while there was nothing but lint inside it now—the gesture was symbolic enough. "I'll work it off."

"What about the loss of tonight's proceeds? I run a *bar*, not a ballroom, you know."

"Knock it off. This is the best way to get Krall back without making more of a mess. Unless you want me to steal it from Serana directly?"

Marcus had the decency to sigh.

"Besides," Logan added, sensing victory, "I'm sure you'll get plenty of business to make up for it—once those rich mortals tonight get a good look at this place and its hole-in-the-wall vibe."

Marcus shrugged and went back to stirring whatever was in that pot of his. "Tell her we only accept cash—but make sure you get Krall. Tonight. No threats, no violence."

"Agreed." Logan rushed back into the bar room and declared, "You can stop panicking. It's all taken care of."

He'd meant it solely as a figure of speech, but when he caught sight of Serana, perched on a barstool, as white as a sheet, he had a feeling that—at least during the few minutes he'd been talking to Marcus—she'd done nothing but panic.

And, as a result, she looked so damn…vulnerable. For the briefest of moments, those gray eyes were soft and wide and —grateful. It threw him off.

"W-What? You mean—"

He nodded. "Consider it done."

Of course, her gratefulness lasted only a second before the ice returned in full.

"I won't pay a penny more than the amount I've already done to secure the rec room."

And they were back to square one.

"Don't worry about it," Logan told her—he meant it too. "You can pay me back another way…"

He advanced before she could react, trapping her body against the bar. When he palmed the front of her pants, he fully intended to check if she still had Krall. Not savor the way she felt pressed against him.

And her scent. Sweet. Soft. Fragrant. His nostrils flared as he inhaled as much of her as he could.

"What the hell do you want?"

He stiffened at the question—this was a perfect moment to voice the truth, *my knife.*

"I want *you*, Serana," he blurted instead. "One night, no strings attached."

What the hell? Logan didn't have long to question his own thinking—was he really that horny he'd risk his freedom, and safety by prolonging his retrieval of Krall?—because he barely saw her palm connect with the side of his face. *Thwack!* It took everything he had to silence a groan as the deliciously sharp pain lanced through his system.

Good God.

Serana used the distraction to wiggle away from him, brandishing her purse as a shield. "Forget it. I'll find someplace else—"

"Wait," Logan called as she headed for the door. "It's too short notice. You'll never find another place by tonight. I'm sorry," he added when she took another step. That stopped her in her tracks, though.

"Then I will pay *in cash*," she said coldly. "How much?"

Tallying all of Marcus' conditions, he voiced a quote, and her eyes threatened to bulge from her head.

"I can't...we can't afford that," she said.

Logan sighed. "Don't worry about it—*seriously*," he insisted, when her eyes narrowed. "Marcus is happy to do it for the clinic. So am I. Give me your contact information, including your number. I'll handle the rest."

Serana still looked skeptical, but she must have been more desperate than he thought because she didn't run. Even more surprising, she pulled out her cell phone and allowed him to program his number into her contacts list while she entered her phone number and address into his phone.

"Are you sure?"

Logan hated the grim suspicion in her voice. Damn, was she *that* used to everyone screwing her over?

"I mean it," he said, meeting her gaze. "But I do want you to answer another question. Nothing sexual, I swear."

She didn't seem convinced. "What?"

"My knife. Did you take it home with you?"

She shivered, her lips parting.

The next second, Mirabelle barged inside, and Serana recoiled away from him as if he had the plague.

"Logan! Please, please tell me Marcus said yes? If not, I'll go back there and beg until he does—"

"It's okay," Logan said as she moved to do just that. "No need for violence. The fundraiser will be held here. You can coordinate everything with Marcus."

Mirabelle beamed in a way that would have let even the most hardened soul know that there was still good left in this world.

"Really? Oh Logan, thank you!" She threw her arms around him and gave him a grateful squeeze.

"Don't thank me," he murmured into her golden hair. "It's not *my* bar."

"Right!" Beaming, she pulled away from him and skipped off to the kitchen to attack Marcus with her gratitude.

He watched her go, more unsettled than he'd been in prison, presented with a rare offer of freedom. The truth of who she really was—to him and to the world—was like a festering sore in the center of his chest that hurt to think on for too long.

He settled with turning his attention to Serana instead. She was watching him. Slowly, her eyes trailed from his face, over to the exiting Mirabelle, and back again.

He wondered what she was thinking—and that scared the hell out of him. He wasn't used to caring about what women wanted or thought or whether they had a venue in which to throw some fancy fundraising party.

To be fair, other women were so much simpler to read. They didn't try so hard. Hide so hard.

Serana Blake was an annoying puzzle that he wanted to solve, shelve, and move on. Though…it certainly didn't help that in the dim light of the bar, her gray eyes almost seemed to glow, enticing him to wonder how else they appear in different situations.

In his bed, for instance.

"Thank you," she said softly, throwing him for another whirlwind loop.

If it weren't for the way the sound of her voice cradled, what he hadn't realized was the beginnings of a throbbing erection, he would have assumed that he had imagined it. The next instant, she was gone, disappearing out into the sunshine that glanced off her dark hair.

It wasn't until she turned the corner that Logan realized he had forgotten all about Krall.

Again.

Damn it. He started after her, but by the time he reached the end of the block, she was already entering the rec center.

A warning prickle on the back of his neck distracted him from the pursuit. He barely managed to turn in time to dodge a black shape rushing for his head.

What the hell?

He reached for Krall only to come up empty-handed. Luckily, his attacker wasn't of the daemon or even mortal variety.

It was a bird, more massive than the typical crow. It cawed loudly, but a shiver wracked Logan's spine as the shrill sound resonated with far more clarity than it should have. He could almost make out actual words. Something like… "Remember your task!"

Birds didn't speak, even in the daemon world. With a hard swallow, he watched it fly off, recognizing exactly what it had been—a missive, sent by those daemon-hunting friends of his. Apparently, they were getting impatient.

And even if he were in a hurry, he didn't exactly have the tool necessary to carry out his task anyway.

He needed Krall, and fast. Tonight, would be his last chance to grab it without having to resort to larceny—and while he was at it, he might as well take care of Mirabelle before his jail breakers came to town to assess his progress.

Easy right?

A lump in his throat warned otherwise, not that he stopped to examine any doubts.

ELEVEN

Serana looked at her reflection and tried her hardest to convince herself that this entire evening wasn't a hopeless cause.

Her dress was too big. She looked like a Vicar's wife with her hair pulled back into a severe bun. Still…

It's for the clinic. One night of socialization couldn't kill her —could it? She tried to put on a brave face as she left the house and climbed into her car.

All in all, the night was saved. Despite the drama at the community center, the fundraiser was still on. After an entire day of moving things over from the rec room, Serana just hoped that no one would mind being crammed into Marcus' bar.

She drove slowly, taking a few more back roads than usual until she couldn't put it off any longer, and arrived at the pub. She parked in an alley along the back of the building and tried her best to smooth her hair before finally heading inside.

In the dim glow of a few lanterns, the place didn't look half bad. Someone had rehung the banners, and the clinic pamphlets neatly lined the bar.

The smells of cooking food greeted her as she set her purse on a stool. She had no idea how Marcus had arranged the various items the caterer had provided, but as long as his services were free, she didn't really care.

Which reminded her that it was only free...because of Logan.

Don't kid yourself, she thought. *Sooner or later, he'll cash in. Hold this over your head. Try and extort something out of you.*

For the moment, she was too desperate to care. This fundraiser was important for the clinic. Vital. Without new funds, their budget would barely last the year—she couldn't fail.

There was too much riding on this.

As far as she was concerned, Logan could have whatever he wanted until this night was over. After that, she wouldn't owe him a damn thing.

Speaking of Logan...

She blinked as he appeared in the doorway that she knew led to the kitchen. He looked good even in a tee and jeans, but tonight, clad in a skintight black shirt and dangerously dark slacks, he looked...

Good enough to eat. Serana flinched as the thought crossed her mind. It didn't help that he held a tray of hors d'oeuvres in one hand while a wicked smile shaped that sensual mouth.

Just survive this night with him, she told herself, gritting her teeth. *Just one night—you can do it.*

As he took her in with one heated look, she doubted it would be so easy.

"Serana." He drew her name out on a rough strain of syllables that made her belly tighten. "You look—"

"Save it," she snapped, holding her purse between them like a weapon. "I'm not interested in you, so just leave me alone."

"I was going to say morbid," Logan murmured, picking a piece of food from the tray, and popping it into his mouth.

Ouch. Serana couldn't keep from flinching. For once, those green eyes weren't glinting with mischief. He looked…angry.

Luckily, Mirabelle arrived a second later, drawing the attention away. Like always, the woman looked marvelous in a confection of white silk.

The rest of the guests began arriving soon after that, and Serana tried her hardest to erase all thoughts of Logan from her mind and just focus on being the perfect smiling host capable of charming rich patrons out of their money.

Unsurprisingly, Mirabelle fit that role better than she did.

That woman certainly knew how to work a room, and Serana didn't even bother to try. Instead, she found herself behind the bar, helping Katie, a clinic volunteer, serve drinks…and watching Logan.

The man was a million-watt bulb with all the charisma of Mirabelle times a thousand. He had women eating out of the palm of his hand and stuffy old men laughing at his jokes.

He was…

Well, to put it bluntly, Serana figured she was the only woman in the world who'd turn him down for sex.

He didn't want you, she told herself as she poured alcohol into a shot glass and handed it off to a man in a suit.

He had wanted something *from* her.

Obviously, the guy was addicted to sex and didn't care who he got it from. Why else would he come after her anyway, and not a woman like Mirabelle—familial relationship aside?

She watched him closely. Waited for him to flirt or eye or tease another woman with the same degree of intensity that he did her.

She waited…

But other than small talk or a few jokes, he never paid anyone more attention than it took to serve them, warm them up enough to open their wallets, and move on.

Serana couldn't understand it. But the few times their eyes met…

There was heat. She couldn't deny it. A desire she'd never felt before—Mark Kell times a thousand. Pressure built between her thighs in an undeniable rhythm.

God, she was going insane.

Impulsively, Serana reached for another shot glass, filled it to the brim with liquid from the bottle still clutched in her hand, and downed it all in one gulp. The harsh, acidic burn snapped her back to her senses, and the longing disappeared, if only briefly.

A wave of dizziness replaced it instead, making her sway on her feet.

"You, okay?" Katie asked with concern.

Serana couldn't even find the strength to nod.

I have to get out of here. Fingers shaking, she made up an excuse about having to use the ladies' room and ducked into the crowd before she did something stupid. Like, try to imagine just what Logan would do to her if she consented to his little bargain.

One night, no strings attached…

She'd been alone for so long. Would she even know what to do, if the man somehow did manage to get her into bed? Though why would she even consider it?

Could it be because of that nightmare involving his knife?

Stop it. Once inside the bathroom, she scrambled into the nearest empty stall. Trembling from head to toe, she sat down on the edge of the toilet seat and just…

Tried to breathe. Steady herself. Anything to regain her composure and push Logan to the back of her mind.

"I'm Serana Blake," she told herself, cradling her face in her hands. "No one will ever be able to break me down. *Ever.*"

Even to her own ears, the words sounded hollow.

She didn't know how long she hid in the stall, but it had to be sometime later when the door opened, and a gaggle of laughing women slipped inside.

Holding her breath, Serana tried to ignore their mindless gossip. They gushed over the men and the abundance of alcohol—of which they all seemed to have had too much of. She'd almost succeeded in tuning them out completely when a sudden change in topic caught her attention.

"…you seen Serana?" someone asked, her voice a little too loud in the enclosed space. If the lisp was anything to go by, then the speaker was probably Rachel, the clinic secretary.

"No," someone said curtly, Sara.

While another person pitched in with a mocking, "You mean the *Ice Queen?*"

Something in the hateful tone—the way they laughed—made Serana lift her head and peek through the narrow slit in the stall.

"She probably left," Sara said softly. "You know she never stays at events long."

"A good thing for us," Rachel added. There was a rush of running water from the faucet and then a slight pause. "She only ever lurks in the shadows anyway. Who'd want to donate to anything when the lead organizer is about as welcoming as Morticia Adams?"

It was a low blow—her family had practically built the clinic from the ground up—but Serana bit her lip against an impulsive reply and just forced herself to listen.

"She's so cold," someone added. "No wonder she never seems to date anyone—"

"Who'd even want to date her?" Rachel pitched in. "She seems like she'd be about as welcoming as an ice cube in bed."

There were a few scattered laughs.

"I saw the waiter sneaking glances at her," Sara interjected. "The blond one with the nice eyes."

Nice, burning emerald eyes Serana could picture clearly.

"Him?" Rachel snorted. "What on earth would someone like *him* want with someone like *her*?"

"Maybe it's a conquest thing?" the third woman wondered.

"Or maybe," Rachel added nastily, "he just has a thing for dogs?"

Serana would have been lying to herself if she denied the jab stung. Just a little. She had always been sensitive about her appearance. Once upon a time, she would have given anything to look as beautiful as Zoe, her stepsister. To have long blond hair and soft hazel eyes…

"I think Sara needs her eyes checked," Rachel declared. "Besides, *that* hottie's coming home with me tonight."

There was a smattering of eager "or me's," as they openly fantasized about how "wonderful" the blond would be in the sack. Finally, they finished up and rejoined the party.

Leaving Serana stuck in that tiny stall in the bathroom. She couldn't move. Couldn't stand. Couldn't do anything but sit and stare and breathe as the first few trickles of tears started to fall.

Damn. It had been so long since she'd allowed herself to cry. Since she'd wallowed in the pain that always seemed to loom at the back of her mind, just waiting to swallow her up. She hadn't even shown emotion at her own father's funeral. Just composure, though no one could have guessed that it was sheer will that had pushed her to show up at all.

She was used to pushing emotions back—shoving her tears deep down to the back of her throat where they couldn't bother anyone.

This time was no different.

She let just one or two more fall before wiping them away with the back of her hand. Suddenly, she climbed to her feet before pure exhaustion could steal her nerve again. The floor seemed to sway beneath her as she stumbled out of the stall and over to the sink, where her tired reflection greeted her with all the warmth of a ghost.

She looked dead. Sallow cheeks made her look hollow, with her hair pulled back so flat that her temples were starting to ache. She'd seen statues with more life.

In fact, the only thing that seemed to hold any shine to it at all was her hair, threatening to break free from its restrictive bun. Fingers shaking, she reached back to unhook the twist of her bun, allowing her hair to spill down over her shoulders to mingle with the plain neckline of her gown.

Now, instead of sad and pathetic, she just looked…frozen. A figure made of ice, impervious to being fucked with.

Or just plainly fucked.

Stop thinking about it, she tried to tell herself. *You're only hurting yourself.*

But it was hard to keep that last cruel piece of gossip from darting around her mind as she pulled open the bathroom door and slipped back out into the main bar.

The party had begun to wind down. The main room, which had seemed packed with people before, was now almost empty except for a few workers like Paul and Robbie, who were busy taking down the banners, and Mirabelle, who stood at the bar, counting out slips of paper that looked to be checks.

Rachel, Sara, and Amanda weren't anywhere to be seen. But Logan was, and somehow that comforted her to know that he hadn't gone skipping off to bed with one of those harpies.

The feeling of relief lasted all of ten seconds until he looked her way with a brief glance that held…

Nothing. No heat. No fire. No heavy undertones of sexual innuendo.

For probably the first time since she'd met him, Logan's expression was carefully blank. She got nothing—not even when he saw her hair, spilling down over her shoulders in wild waves.

"Serana! There you are!"

It was like all of the water being sucked out of a bathtub after the drain plug was pulled, as she forced herself to break the eye contact and face Mirabelle, who stood excitedly over her shoulder.

"Look!" the woman exclaimed, waving a stack of what seemed to be a mixture of cash and checks beneath her chin. "It's enough!—more than enough. We're all set!"

Serana allowed herself a tired smile. The entire evening might have sucked for her, but at least something good had come out of it for everyone else.

More than good, she realized as Mirabelle voiced the total they'd collected.

"That's not even all of it," the blond went on excitedly. "We even got promises to donate equipment, supplies—whatever we need!"

"That's great," Serana said truthfully. With this event out of the way, she could finally have a shot at a night of peaceful sleep.

If, she could sleep at all.

"Excuse me," she found herself murmuring to Mirabelle before turning away to head to another corner of the room. Near the space where a certain someone leaned over the bar, trying his hardest to pretend that she didn't exist. "You all can leave…I'll finish up."

"You sure?" Mirabelle sounded skeptical.

Robbie and Paul, however, seemed about ready to rip up the banner they held and bolt from the door.

"I'm sure," she said quietly, inclining her head to the exit. "You guys have earned it."

Mirabelle looked like she might refuse, while the others finished up their tasks and left with hasty goodbyes.

"Go," Serana insisted, feeling a touch of gratitude for one of the few people who seemed to actually *want* to be her friend, for whatever reason. "I mean it. Just come in extra early tomorrow to help me process *that*." She nodded toward the stack of donations in the woman's hand.

Mirabelle nodded, eyes sparkling in a way that let Serana know she was dangerously close to incurring one of the woman's infamous hugs.

"Go, I'll be fine."

Mirabelle hesitated for just a second longer, before she turned back to the bar and grabbed her purse. "Good night, Serana," she called before heading to the door. "I'll be sure to drop these off at your office."

Serana barely heard her. Barely heard the bell chime above the door as the last employee left. She just stood there, dazed in the center of the room, watching as Logan cleaned and stacked glasses at the bar, with his back firmly set against her.

Had he given up on his little conquest mission already? The thought annoyed her for some reason. Obviously, what he wanted from her could just as easily be gained from someone else.

Though, he hadn't left with Amanda or Rachel. And there had probably been other women to proposition him, she knew—she doubted that anyone had been able to take their eyes off him tonight. She hadn't.

And for some reason, he had wanted her.

Maybe it was a fetish? Logic told her that men like Logan weren't used to sticking around—maybe she just seemed like the least amount of risk. Not dating material, obviously, but okay enough for a one-night stand.

And maybe a one-night stand was all she wanted? All she needed. She could still remember the feel of his mouth on hers…

The memory alone shrouded her in heat. She hardly even noticed when a massive man with shaggy black hair appeared in the doorway leading to the kitchen.

"You clean up," he called gruffly. It took Serana a minute to realize that he wasn't speaking to her.

"Whatever," Logan called from the counter. "Just leave the door unlocked for me, okay?"

"Sure thing. Just… Make sure you tie up any loose ends, got it?" With that, Marcus turned away, but not before giving her a genuine smile that seemed to transform his stern mouth. "Goodnight."

"G-Goodnight," she stammered, but he was already gone.

Leaving her alone…with Logan.

He still hadn't turned to look at her. Not so much as a glance from over his shoulder, but Serana forced her chin into the air as she walked over to him anyway.

"Logan," she called tentatively at his back.

He didn't react, but his shoulders stiffened at the sound of her voice.

So, he *was* ignoring her then.

Unperturbed, she approached as he leaned against the edge of the counter. He didn't turn to face her, but she heard his breath catch as if her closeness interfered with his ability to draw in air. Though, he didn't seem to *breathe* at all as she allowed her body to drape over the back of his, suddenly boneless.

A part of her screamed in alarm. *What are you doing?* It was hard to feel that way for very long. Admired from afar, his body was impressive. Felt up close…

Serana had to bite her lip just to keep from groaning at the hard, firm sensation of him. Slowly, she brought her hands up over each of his shoulder blades, shivering in tune to the shudder that ran through him at her touch.

"What the hell are you doing?" His voice was so guttural. One part annoyance, two parts lust with a little bit of confusion sprinkled in. The swirl of emotions in him was so intoxicatingly delicious that Serana would have laughed had she had any breath left in her chest. Instead, she reached down to cup the firm ridges shaping the back of his pants…

Goodness, was every part of the man rock solid?

As her fingers lowered, he released a growl that made her hair stand on end. Without warning, he turned, catching her by both wrists.

Dark with dizzying confusion, those green eyes bore into hers. "What are you…what…"

What *was* she doing? She had no damn idea, but it didn't feel wrong. For once, she didn't have to be hard, ruthless Serana. She merely reacted, and stood on tiptoe to press her mouth against his.

His lips were so soft. The feel of them against her own made her mind go blank. Evaporate. She trailed her tongue along his bottom lip, marveling at the firmness like the soft give of a peach.

Logan stood frozen for all of five seconds before the shock went away. His breath caught. Then, he lunged against her, crushing her back, tongue jabbing deep into her mouth, scraping the tops of her teeth.

God. Liquid heat curled and unfolded in her belly, slipping down to coat the center of her thighs. She wasn't the only one—she could feel that hard budge rubbing against her abdomen again. This time, she leaned into him, embracing the molten-hot feel.

Who had caused him to be so solid? she wondered. *Amanda or Rachel?*

She didn't care.

Hungrily she kissed him, matching his tongue stroke for stroke. He pressed her against him, hands reaching down to cinch her waist, pulling her against the hardness of his thighs. She could fully feel the outline of what had to be an erection now, nudging her belly as firm as stone.

Shaking, Serana reached up into the thickness of his hair. Her mouth went dry at the feel—so *so* much softer than what she'd imagined in her dreams. *Silk…* She raked her fingers through it, at the same time bringing her other hand down between them to cup that hard—

Logan hissed, pulling back from her to bury his mouth near the crook of her shoulder. "Don't tease me," he growled against her ear, reaching down to wrench her hand away. "Don't—"

"No." Serana didn't know how she managed to speak at all. Her body was on fire, mind numb, urging her to shuck off his grip and reach down to curl her fingers around him again.

His entire body rippled. A groan tore from his throat, as he jerked, straining against her fingertips. Serana stroked him boldly with her fingers, longing to take him fully in her hand. Longing to...

"What are you—" His voice was a moan that scratched her skin, barely even legible. "What are you doing?"

What *was* she doing? Her voice shook as she tried to put the desire into words—even as the answer came to her quick and sudden—*losing control for once.*

"I want you, Logan," she croaked huskily. "I want you... One night only, no strings attached."

TWELVE

Logan's shock lasted a second. More than enough time to reach beneath her dress and tear off her panties before she could change her mind. She watched him, her head tipped back, dark hair spilling down her shoulders…

He tried to remember something. Something important, involving Krall and logistics and daemon prison.

Ah, hell. The second his hand brushed her thigh—and she shuddered in response—he forgot everything but this.

Her.

With a growl, he lifted her onto the edge of the bar and muscled his way between those slender thighs. Her head tilted back as he dropped a handful of lacy black panties onto the floor.

Her legs spread further for him, and a suffocating sense of rightness took over. Blotted out all shred of common sense

—like the fact that it was probably *not* a good idea to fuck a woman over the counter of his brother's bar.

Respect for Marcus was the only thought he had before curling those pale legs around his waist, and stumbling back behind the counter into the narrow grove where they stored the liquor. There, he propped her against the sink, loving the way she sighed as her bare ass touched the cold metal.

Logan dragged a hand through her hair, pulling her forward to kiss her again. A searching, wrenching kiss that made the heat flare straight down until he just couldn't take it.

As if it had a will of its own, his free hand was already sliding between them, brushing her once before releasing himself from the painful confines of his zipper. Like steel, he felt himself spring for her, straining through the cotton of his boxers.

At the back of his mind, he tried to remember the plan he'd had in his mind for what he'd do to her. Tease her, taunt her, make her come before he even entered her. Then tease her again…

But, at the feel of her in his arms, all those thoughts went away beneath the need to have her. Any way he could.

Now.

He shoved his pants down one-handed, leaving them around his ankles, before dragging down his own boxers.

She shivered watching him, gray eyes heavy-lidded, and Logan knew that if he didn't enter her in five seconds, he'd come all over the floor.

Fuck it. He made a fervent promise to himself to make her come anyway, before gripping his cock with one hand and guiding it to her entrance with the other.

The moist heat greeting him was a shock. *Damn.*

At first, to slow himself down—give him more time—he only eased his head against her, nudging her tight folds until her legs parted a little more with a sigh, and he could begin to push inside.

Heat. Stifling. Silky. Gloriously wet.

Those were the only words Logan could think of to describe the feel of her slick channel, holding him tight. It had been a long, long while since she'd had a man within her—he could tell. But even so, she opened easily as he rammed himself deep with a sudden thrust.

Her moan scratched at his ear, fingers digging deep, scraping along his shoulder blades. The burning pain made Logan slide a hand beneath her, cupping the smooth curve of her ass, protecting her from the cold metal beneath her as he let go and just rocked into her.

He didn't know how to go slow or be gentle. Didn't exactly *want* to. With every thrust, his hips ground harshly over hers, pushing himself deeper, but she only groaned, head tipping forward to rest on his shoulder.

And it was just lightning after that. Hot, white, that light licked at the edges of his vision as he took her. Hard. Fast. Slow and steady. Then, harder…

She was molten in no time. As his pace quickened, her nails turned into claws, ripping down the sides of his back, probably drawing blood, and he just pounded into her, giving her all he had.

He was close, feeling a climax building throughout his skin when her cool fingers cradled the bottom of his chin, tilting his face down to meet hers. Those gray eyes were wide, open pools of silver. Drowning him, suffocating him until there was nothing left but raw, primal lust that had him snarling as he rolled his hips and rammed into her over and over and over...

"Logan!" His name, a gasp from her mouth, was the last thing he was aware of before a searing heat licked him from the inside out, and he was lost. He was seconds from bursting, breaking apart when one cold fact nudged at the back of his brain like a stick of lethal dynamite.

Ah, fuck.

THIRTEEN

Was it over? The thought nearly brought tears to her eyes as his last desperate thrust was followed by a long moment of shuddering stillness.

Good God, she wanted more—*needed* more. She moaned her disappointment as Logan withdrew from her body, leaving her so close to the edge it made her entire body quake.

The edge of what?—she had no idea. All she knew was that if he didn't sink back inside of her, she'd go insane.

"Logan." Blindly, she reached for him, desperate to pull him back. "Please…"

"Fuck," she heard him grunt. "No condom."

Oh. A semblance of common sense returned to her like a one-two punch. All along, he'd been inside of her without a condom. Judging by the harshness of his breath, if he hadn't stopped when he did…

He could have gotten her pregnant. The realization made some bit of gratitude unfurl in her chest—most men wouldn't have cared about the consequences of having their fun in the moment of passion. Though, as she still felt him between her thighs, it was so hard not to just say fuck it. Let him ride her bare and take the risk.

She was so damn *raw*. The need to have him inside of her, any way she could, was instinctive. Voice shaking, she called out to him. "Find one."

"I'm trying," he hissed in response, though she could tell he was just as aching as she was. Maybe more so. His erection twitched against her thigh as if desperate to be back inside, plunging in and out at a heart-stopping rhythm.

You can't raise a baby, she told herself—the only thing holding her back from arching her hips and urging him back within her again.

From nearby, she could hear the thud and rustle of drawers being opened, rummaged ruthlessly through, and slammed shut. Not even a minute later, he released his breath on one harsh word, "Fuck. You'd think the bastard would at least keep a box or two in the damn bar…"

There were no condoms then. For a moment, such an intense wave of disappointment engulfed Serana—she had to suck in air just to keep from being swallowed by it. It figured that the one time she decided to give in. Have a little fun. The bastard forgot to bring condoms.

"Upstairs?" she asked, not recognizing the hopeful tone in her voice—borderline pleading. From what she'd guessed, he and Marcus lived in an apartment above the pub. If Logan was as much of a playboy as he seemed, then he must have had a whole stash of condoms there.

In the darkness, she saw Logan shake his head. "Not me," he grunted reluctantly. "Haven't gotten around to it, and Marcus is…celibate."

Just her luck.

There was a 24-hour convenience store just up the street, she knew. Would he be willing to trudge out into the darkness just for sex? *Oh hell yes,* the fire in his eyes claimed. He'd trudge through a field of thorns just to finish what he'd started.

But could she wait? Already, she was so damn close…

Logan's eyes flashed, and as if reading her mind, he slid a hand beneath her, forcing her hips into a slight arch.

"Just…trust me," he urged, before sliding a single finger deep.

Serana nearly bucked off the damn counter, heedless of the hand tethering her down like an anchor, holding her steady, his finger twisted, sending sparks shooting behind her eyes.

It wasn't the same as being filled to the brim by his cock, but…

The warm sensation of any part of him inside her made her groan out low into the air, gasping as he pulled her closer, pressing his mouth against her ear.

"Serana," the growl teased her as his finger made way for another, and then another…

"Fuck, you're so *tight*," he moaned as she cried out. "I can't stand it—" He broke off with a groan, bucking her hard against the counter while his erection stabbed at her thigh.

Impulsively, Serana reached down between them, sliding him into her hand, cradling the thick heat as stiff as steel. Her fingers stroked him, matching the devious way his own twisted and rubbed inside of her until her breaths hitched into hoarse sobs groaned out against his shoulder.

He was gasping as well. Groaning and growling as his hand shoved deeper with every answering touch.

Though he never truly entered her, Serana could *feel* the throbbing length of him pressing against the folds of her flesh, blocked only by his own hand as it slid in and out of her. Then, before she knew it, he slid the pad of his thumb hard against a small nub of flesh, nestled near the center of her core, and *she* instinctively flicked a finger along the slick, wet head of him…

Explosive.

They shouted together, bodies jerking and thrusting into one another like crashing waves of a tempest ocean until…

She lost her mind. Lost all thought. All sense.

Nothing made sense. Nothing but heat and fire and how damn right it felt to scream her throat sore as white flooded her vision, and everything in the world went perfect for just the briefest of moments.

As if from far away, she heard herself break, cry out his name. Loud enough to feel him shudder, cock twitching as he came against the inside of her thigh.

And then there was just silence, broken only by the harsh sounds of panting as color returned, forcing Serana to face just what the hell she'd done.

FOURTEEN

Good Gods, *she was beautiful.* He wasn't being superficial, by referring to her body or a specific part of her anatomy, either.

Just *her.*

Viewed in the dim lighting of the closed bar, Serana Blake looked absolutely beautiful. Logan sighed as he took her all in—black hair a mess, skin flushed, dress bunched up around her thighs.

If only he had a rubber sheath to slip on so that he could show her what a night with him was truly meant to be. Even with her pleasured moans echoing off the inside of his skull, he still wanted her. Still ached for her, and that scared the living hell out of him.

It wasn't real sex, he tried to tell himself. A brief taste of the warmth of her body and some hasty foreplay didn't count against his one rule.

He could have her again, guilt free. Though, he couldn't exactly have her camp out in the back of Marcus' bar all night.

Gently, he lifted her from the sink and pulled her along to fish her ripped panties from the floor.

He paused only to switch off the lights and lock the front door before trudging up the back staircase, guiding Serana by her wrist.

She didn't move. Not even when he eased open the door to Marcus' apartment, trying his hardest not to make a sound. Thankfully, his brother wasn't anywhere to be seen in the small kitchen. The living room either—but the door to his bedroom was firmly closed.

Leaving no one to witness as Logan led Serana into the bathroom and set her down on the toilet seat before he started to strip.

In the workings of his logic, it wasn't breaking any rules to undress her. Especially not when she had the product of his release smeared all over the inside of her thigh. He pulled her dress over her head and took a second to recall what had gone through his head the first time he'd seen her in it. The conservative design had unexpectedly hugged her body in a way that had him on edge all night, fighting to ignore her presence. In the end, he'd failed miserably, and with a sigh, he balled the fabric in a fist and tossed it into the small trashcan Marcus kept beside the sink, along with the torn remains of those black panties.

When he returned to Serana, she let him pull her into the warmth of the shower. The water felt like a blessing over his skin, and from her low moan, he could tell that it did wonders for her too.

With her leaning against him, he lathered up a washrag and worked the soapy mixture all over her skin. Surprisingly, there was nothing sensual in his touch. Just a desire to help her clean—and maybe get a sight of the body that had taunted him like no other.

She wasn't quite so shapeless beneath all that boxy clothing. In fact, she was perfectly lean, with her skin taut in all the right places. Not to mention her breasts which, while small, perfectly molded to his hands.

When a dusky, pink nipple became bared as he washed the lather away, Logan couldn't keep himself from swiping a thumb against it, and she shuddered, her gray eyes meeting his.

Those damn eyes nearly did him in, and he switched off the water before he could make a fool of himself by soiling another part of her body.

She waited patiently on the edge of the tub as he darted into his room for an old pair of sweats. With a bit of guilt, he pictured her ruined underwear—but, hey, he wasn't exactly opposed to having her wear his clothes with nothing but *her* underneath.

Even the thought made him feel…

Confined in his own clothing.

Especially when she pulled on his old tee and sweatpants without complaint. Then, she dutifully followed him into the narrow room Marcus let him use while he was in town and climbed into the bed.

He remained standing, swallowing a lump in his throat at the sight of her.

"Logan?" Her voice was a whisper, but he stiffened at the sound regardless. He was beginning to realize that only she had that power. One word, and every muscle in his body tightened. Then he reluctantly returned to her side.

"Yes?" His hand was in her hair before he could stop himself, spreading the strands over his pillow.

"No strings means we don't talk after this, right?"

In theory. He shrugged by way of answer, but internally he was already coming up with plenty of loopholes around his own personal philosophy. Talking wasn't sexual, right? Therefore, no harm, no foul if he happened to see her on the street and responded to a greeting.

Unless, of course, he was already back in Hell, having carried out his task.

"I want you to tell me something," she whispered, interpreting his silence as consent. "Who was she? The woman who made you…"

"Avoid relationships?" he finished for her. "The truth is, there was no woman. I'm just not the commitment type."

"Liar." Her eyes were swollen in the moonlight filtering in through the room's lone window, and Logan's breath caught. "You're afraid, just like I am. You let someone in—you risk them hurting you. Ergo, you keep them at an arm's distance. Do you want to know my reason?"

He said nothing, but she continued regardless, drawing in a steadying breath. "A few years ago... I had a little pill problem," she said, stumbling over the phrasing. He recognized the hitch in her voice and suspected what she'd held back—in reality, her "little" problem had nearly cost her everything, much like his venture into thievery had thrown his own life into turmoil. He didn't take her words for granted. Why confide in him at all? He didn't know. "It almost ruined my life, and it's why I can't get a job anywhere outside of Meyweather. My father wasn't understanding, and when I came back...I think it made things worse. When he died, it was a wake-up call, and I finally got clean. Now you know."

He swallowed hard, finding himself leaning in closer. "Could you let someone like me in?"

She took her time appraising him with those endless eyes. Against her dark hair, the silvery hue struck a stunning contrast.

"No," she said finally. "I think I'd wind up getting hurt in the end."

And she had no damn idea. "You're right," he agreed, still frozen beside her on the edge of the bed. "I'm no addict, but I still manage to fuck up everything with anyone who has ever had the misfortune of seeing something in me other than, well… A fuck up."

Marcus was included on that list, and perhaps even Mirabelle. Much like the sole weapon his mother gifted to him as a child, his only purpose was to harm and destroy. Hurt.

His recurring nightmare was more like a figurative explanation for why he was the way he was—a self-contained ball of hellfire destroying anyone caught in his path.

"At least you're honest," Serana said sleepily. Did that bother her? He couldn't tell. She was asleep soon after, and Logan almost felt guilty for tiring her out. Especially when they'd done so little.

Judging from the dark shadows beneath her eyes, she might have just been running low on sleep. He tried not to think of why as he left her there, unconcerned about Marcus or the fact that he had a woman he'd promised only a one-night stand sleeping in his bed.

He tried not to think about anything as he headed out into the darkness of nightfall, doing what he did best.

Leaving.

FIFTEEN

Serana felt cold as she peeled her eyes open against a swath of gray morning light. Not in a bad way—like the frigid chill of her own house—but that refreshing cool that tickled the skin after a moment spent too close to a heater.

She felt well rested, too. Probably for the first time in…ever. Maybe it had something to do with the soft, clean sheets beneath her? Or the mattress that was so much more comfortable than her own?

Yep, she realized, wrenching her eyes open. She was definitely *not* in her own bed.

In fact, she wasn't in her house. The plain white walls of a small, but clean room served to reinforce her confusion. There wasn't a piece of expensive, unnecessary furniture in sight.

Definitely not in Kansas anymore.

Cautiously, she pulled herself upright, shucking off the heavy blankets. Someone had draped them over her—a realization that should have triggered more alarm than it did. *Oh.* As she blinked against a stream of blinding daylight, it all started coming back. In rapid snatches, she recalled the bar. Logan. Being pressed against the sink. Being...

Holy, mother of. She cradled her face in her hands, aware of loose hair and a plain shirt she wore instead of her dress. They were proof of the horrifying explanation forming in her mind.

She had had sex with Logan—or come close to it, at least. Sure enough, deep within her body, she felt a soft, faint ache as if she'd fully exercised muscles she hadn't used in a long time. Not only that, but she'd gone a step further and revealed her past addiction, or at least the sanitized parts that evaded any responsibility for her father's death.

Though, the funny thing was...

Shouldn't she have felt shame? Disgust? Hated herself?

She certainly had after her little tryst with Mark Kell. Tears of guilt had stung her eyes as she'd cleaned herself later that night in the shower, knowing deep in her heart that the desire he'd claimed to feel for her had been false. Also, pretty convinced that, despite the rumors floating around the high school, sex pretty much sucked.

But now...

All she could think about when it came to the act was doing it *again*. With Logan—preferably someplace more comfortable than on the sink. This bed, maybe? *Yes…* It made something hot prickle in her belly to even think about what it would feel like to have him pressing her down against the mattress.

One night only, remember? a part of her chimed in. *No strings attached.* His promise played over and over in her mind as she braced her hands on either side of her to hold herself steady.

Though, did last night count as far as his promise of no-strings fun went? Technically, he hadn't even been inside her the whole time. Not when it really counted.

Still, she couldn't deny the experience had been socks-blown-off-pray-to-God-and-hold-on-for-dear-life amazing.

Or maybe that was just the edge of alcohol talking—she had taken a shot last night after all. Despite her father's genes, she was a pathetic lightweight, but she certainly didn't feel in the throes of a hangover. Instead, she just felt…

Used. Gloriously, achingly, satisfyingly used. The sensation hummed throughout her entire body as she finally stood and faced the room's only window.

It wasn't even noon yet—still early morning, but with a curse, Serana tried to guess just how early. If she didn't show up at the clinic on time, she wouldn't put it past Mirabelle to go breaking down the door of her house to find her.

If she hadn't already.

Time to go.

She hastily made the bed, replacing the dark blue comforter. Someone had placed her shoes and purse near the door, but her dress wasn't in sight. Or her panties, for that matter, she realized with a shiver once the inside of her thighs chafed from the fabric of the sweatpants someone had dressed her in.

Logan…

She just hoped that his no-strings-attached bit didn't apply to his clothes as she hefted her purse over her shoulder and tiptoed from the room with her heels clutched in one hand. The small hallway of an apartment greeted her, leading into a modest living room that opened onto a decent-sized kitchen. Serana vaguely remembered the way, recalling memories of following Logan through the darkness.

It wasn't dark now. Bright daylight spilled through the windows, perfectly illuminating the figure who stood in the kitchen with his back turned to her, cooking something on the stove.

It took her mind all of five seconds to register that the man with his bulk and dark, black hair wasn't Logan. Neither did he seem to realize that she was there.

Great. Serana froze. Was there some kind of protocol she should follow?

Ignore him? Speak? Climb out from the fire escape?

She hesitated before taking another cautious step.

"Good morning." The deep greeting shocked her so much she almost screamed. The reflex of politeness saved her.

"G-Good morning," she blurted out hoarsely.

Marcus nodded in reply without turning around. Something in the set of his broad shoulders, visible from beneath the cut of a white wife-beater, told her that the good mood was all just an act.

He was pissed. A fairly understandable emotion if you happened to find a strange, half-dressed woman sneaking out of your house during breakfast.

"Second door to the left," he said in that rumbling grumble while gesturing to a set of doors just off the living room. "That will take you straight to the alley, though you're perfectly welcome to eat first—"

"That's fine!" Serana blurted, nearly falling over in her rush to get to the door. "Thank you!"

"No problem. Oh, and Serana?"

Completely mortified, Serana forced herself to pause with one foot through the doorway. "Yes?"

"If you happen to see Logan at all..." Marcus' deep tenor dropped an octave. "Tell him he's a dead man."

"Will do." As she darted from the apartment, she almost felt bad for Logan.

Almost.

CHAPTER

SIXTEEN

Logan spent the morning wandering the streets, lost in the fog of his thoughts—though aware enough to side-eye every bird that flew too close.

None turned out to be another messenger, though he wished one had, if only to give him a much-needed kick in the ass.

So much for his supposed fresh start in the mortal world. Serana Blake was too much of a distraction, though he doubted his Shael heritage had much to do with it. A box of brand-spanking-new condoms was in his pants pocket, but for some reason, he wasn't in a hurry to return to Marcus' and finish where he'd left off with her.

It wasn't like he didn't want to. He *wanted* to, alright. But she'd looked so damn peaceful sleeping in his bed that he loathed the idea of waking her up just for sex.

Weird. He could rationalize it as basic compassion rather than something more tender. After all, he knew firsthand just how painful it could be to go without sleep. After his ordeal in Arcaneum, he'd slept for a week—and if anyone had dared to wake him, he probably would have killed them.

Another reason for his reluctance was that, unfortunately for him, Serana probably had the one weapon capable of ending his life. Krall was still out there, his supposed reason for pursuing her in the first place.

And what had he done? Fuck the whole thing up by letting her proposition him in the pub. By letting lust overtake common sense and self-preservation—which was something he had never done.

He may have been part Shael, but he'd always managed to put himself above the desires of his cock.

Back to business, he thought, steeling his resolve. It was time to get his blade before someone, or something, used his lapse in judgment to cause some hell.

Thankfully, it didn't take long to find where Serana lived, thanks to the contact information she'd innocently provided during the hasty arrangement of the fundraiser. The place was in a shrouded section of town that overlooked the main street from a high hill. The houses there seemed like miniature castles, unwelcoming to any visitors.

Not surprisingly, the Blake house was the tallest and coldest of them all. The sight gave Logan shivers. Actual shivers ran down his spine as he pictured Serana living inside such a place.

No wonder she was so frigid…

He suspected his mother's fortress had more charm. Still, he started down the paved walkway leading to the front of the house and knocked just once.

When he didn't get an answer, he settled for testing the doorknob, unsurprised to find it locked. The fact might have deterred someone else. Luckily for Logan, daemons weren't exactly built to shy away from illegal activity. All it took was a little burst of energy shot through his palm, and the door opened easily.

The narrow foyer beyond it looked about as welcoming as a graveyard crypt. Dark wallpaper and wood paneling threatened to close him in from all sides, paired with a stench of unwelcome energy that permeated the air like a bad smell.

His first thought wasn't of Krall, but of her. He hated the idea of Serana living alone in this place. Even with sunlight through the large windows, the atmosphere seemed to smother all feelings of joy. Happiness. Hope.

His torture chamber held more cheer. A part of him wanted to explore further, venture up those mahogany stairs in search of her room. Maybe there he'd find a bit of warmth? Something he could use to crack that icy outer shell and reveal whoever lay in wait underneath?

But…

First things first, he needed to find Krall.

His palm itched, aching to hold the blade again, and it was with a feeling of impatience that he sent out a few tendrils of daemonic energy, calling the blade to him. It was a risk using such magic outside of Hell—much like drawing on a battery that had a limited amount of juice left. Too much, and he'd put himself out of commission for days.

Anxiously, he waited for the sharp pinch in his gut that would confirm the blade was near, beckoning to his call.

He waited…

And got nothing. Not even a flicker.

What the hell?

If Serana hadn't taken Krall, then all of the nasty possibilities made his stomach ache. It was strange though…

He knew in his gut Krall was there—could sense it. Almost as if…the blade was intentionally blocking him somehow. As if it didn't *want* to be found, not by him anyway.

"Krall, where the fuck are you?" Logan hissed, forsaking stealth. Curling his fingers into a fist, he brandished it and tugged on a chain of daemon energy so hard the entire room quivered beneath his feet.

This time he felt the distinctive tendril of magic that signaled Krall…

Before it faded as suddenly as a candle being snuffed.

What. The. Fuck?

Logan adjusted his posture, holding out both hands before him as he reached deep into his limited well of power. No more restraint—he didn't hold anything back, filling every cell with the desire for his blade.

"Krall, you piece of shit," he snarled. "Harken to me!"

He got another flare. Just a tiny taste of the blade's power before it puttered out. This time, though, he sensed the retreat was deliberate. There was no other explanation—Krall was *intentionally* clamping down on its power to stay hidden.

A non-verbal *fuck you* if there ever was one.

Unbelievably confused, Logan tore a hand through his hair and glanced around the narrow room as if expecting to find the knife hiding in plain sight. He'd had the blade since he was a kid—for the longest time, it had been his sole possession. Something that no one could ever take from him.

Never had Krall shielded itself from him, or ignored his call. Even while he'd suffered in Arcaneum, the familiar energy of that knife had been like a stabilizing hand through it all, allowing him to survive the ordeal with most of his mind intact.

He had never even heard of a daemon blade not wanting to be found by its master. At least not without a shit-ton of dark, twisted magic crafted by a very skilled mage.

Or a cult of crazy daemon hunters who wanted him to cut his sister using that very weapon. Had they done something to it? Or, had a band of apocalypse-worshiping daemons used a beautiful human as a decoy to steal his blade before he could ever carry out his task?

No, that was far-fetched, even for a life like his. As frosty as she was, Serana Blake didn't exactly seem like the type to dabble in the dark arts, or to possess a container capable of shielding daemonic energy.

Which meant that his damn blade—the one thing capable of ending his life, owned since childhood, didn't want to be found.

Annoyance had him gritting his teeth so harshly his jaw ached. His fingers curled in and out of fists, desperate to hit something. On impulse, he scanned the room a second time, and a glass bookcase caught his eye.

Think of Marcus, he told himself while gingerly propping the case open instead of smashing it apart like he longed to do.

Simple and clean had never really been his style. Still, he tried to rein himself in as he carefully inspected the numerous, expensive things in the Blake house.

Good God, did they only collect priceless junk? Store it all on fancy shelves and behind glass cases just to look at?

As a kid, he'd grown up with virtually nothing, but he'd never wished for this kind of wealth. Money just made people a target, and this place—occupied by one lone woman—would have been a thief's paradise. Among the countless figurines and expensive junk, however, he didn't find Krall. Not a glint of metal.

Where the fuck had she put it?

He turned on his heel, continuing through a set of large glass doors that partitioned the room off from what appeared to be an office. A thick mahogany desk dominated the center, surrounded by more bookshelves.

Something made Logan head straight for it. He tore through the drawers and rummaged through a stack of stray documents.

Nothing.

He was ready to give up and move onto another room, when something drew his notice to the base of the desk. Crouching, he found a metal safe tucked against the far corner.

Bingo.

As he reached for it, the hairs on the back of his neck stood on end. Warily, he looked up and found himself staring into a pair of watchful gray eyes.

"Can I help you with something?" Serana asked breathlessly, standing in the doorway of the study, still wearing his clothes.

SEVENTEEN

It felt like an eternity before Serana reached the privacy of her car. Without caring how she looked, she dropped her purse and shoes on the passenger's seat and drove barefoot.

It felt good, in a way. The icy surface was like a well-placed slap, shocking some common sense back into her brain.

She could still feel Logan all over her. His wickedly soft fingers brushing her skin. His mouth on her throat. On hers.

It didn't help any that she wore his clothes. She'd shower and send his borrowed sweats back as soon as she got home. Strangely, a part of her almost dreaded what that meant. Their fling was over and done with. Though, how ironic was it that her first good night's sleep in years had come in the form of a stranger's bed?

The simple fact that Logan had bothered to clean her up, find her new clothes, and put her to bed at all left a bad taste in her mouth—one she knew could never be erased by her toothbrush.

It was almost too soon that she arrived at her father's house. She waited until she only had ten minutes left to get ready for work before Mirabelle would come charging after her.

Even that didn't seem long enough.

With an overwhelming sense of desperation, she unlocked the door leading from the garage into the kitchen and squared her shoulders against that suffocating chill.

Her goal was to run upstairs and shower as quickly as possible. She was mere paces from the staircase when she froze.

Heat. It was faint, just a prickle of warmth along her skin as if someone had had the furnace on blast for just a second before switching it off. A strange smell tinged the air as well. Sharp, like honey, spice, and cloves…

It took a second for Serana's mind to process the meaning—someone was in her house.

Her throat went dry. What should she do? Was the intruder still there, waiting for her to come back? Her father had many enemies. Had one of them tried to one-up the old man now that he was dead?

Calling the police would be the smart thing to do. Instead, she tiptoed down the hallway, holding her breath. The phone was close enough, but something made her turn her head, seeing a figure moving within the study beyond the living room.

Right near the gun safe.

She reacted purely on impulse and crept closer while reaching automatically for a heavy glass statue of Apollo that rested on the mantel. As she neared the glass doors, hefting the sculpture in one hand, she braced herself to attack...

And what? She had no fucking clue. Her palms felt slick as she strained her eyes to make out the figure hunched over her father's desk.

They were tall—massively so with broad shoulders that seemed chiseled from bronze, tousled blond hair, and green eyes...

Holy Shit.

She set the glass statue down on a nearby end table as shock lanced through her like a vice.

Logan? In her house? Looking like a living, breathing incarnation of Apollo himself...but why?

She meant to ask him. Put on a good show and demand what the hell he was doing, searching through the pile of junk on her father's old desk. She *meant* to.

But, as she stood there drinking him in, her mind sort of went blank, and she just watched him instead.

Watching the curve of his shoulders flex beneath his T-shirt as he stooped low to rummage through a drawer before closing it and moving on to another. Obviously, he was looking for something, but it wasn't until she saw him bend down for the gun safe that she remembered his knife.

She must have shifted, or made a noise in the back of her throat because his head jerked up, and he noticed her finally. She tried to ignore how her body quivered as she saw him, dressed casually in a fresh pair of jeans, that hair freshly tousled.

He broke into your house, she told herself. *You should be threatening to call the police, trying to kick him out—not hoping he'll turn around so that you can get a good look at just how well he fits those jeans.*

She shook her head, hoping to clear her thoughts, but it didn't work. When she opened her mouth, instead of demanding an explanation, she just brushed her gaze over those smoldering eyes and blurted, "Can I help you with something?"

His jaw dropped. Literally fell open to reveal a mouth full of straight white teeth and a pink tongue cupped in the center of it all. But not from shock.

Judging from the look in those green eyes, Serana could tell that his reaction had more to do with the fact that she wasn't wearing a bra beneath his white T-shirt than the whole instance of him being inside her house.

Instinctively, she crossed her arms over her chest, cursing the deep chill that seemed to constantly fill the place no matter how high she turned up the thermostat. The motion seemed to shock some sense back into Logan, who lurched to his feet.

"Serana…" He ran a hand through his hair. "Did you sleep okay?"

Huh?

The line of questioning threw her off, and she answered without thinking. "I slept fine. Thanks…"

It wasn't the question that puzzled her, but the *way* he asked it. Full of sincerity. As if he gave a damn.

The shock softened her resolve just a tiny bit, his apparent intrusion aside.

"What are you doing here?" She placed her hands on her hips, hoping that it made up for the lack of anger in her tone.

Logan shrugged. "I thought I'd stop by."

"While I was asleep?" Her eyes narrowed as she noticed how his gaze kept flickering back to the gun safe.

Son of a bitch.

"If this is about your stupid knife," she called, moving toward him, "then you could have just asked for it. *Not* resort to larceny."

That was more like it. Now she sounded icy, cold, and one hundred percent in control again. No more of that awkwardness.

Logan shifted out of her way, and she crouched, opening the safe. Ignoring the multitude of guns, she reached for the knife still wrapped in her nightshirt.

"Here," she spat at Logan—though she didn't hand the blade to him just yet. Instead, she set the bundle on the desk and unwrapped it. She couldn't resist running a finger along the edge of the blade one final time.

Whoa. Had it always felt like that? Warm. Pulsing. Alive to the touch?

She gripped the hilt and lifted it. Immediately, fire jolted through her arm, and she jumped, forced to grab the desk with her free hand.

"Serana?" She barely heard Logan speak. The next second, his hand was on her wrist. His eyes, however, were solely focused on the knife.

"Thank you," he said softly. "I've been looking everywhere for...*it*." He seemed to stop himself from referring to it by something else. *A name*, Serana suspected.

One she knew so surely it was as if the word had been engraved into the inside of her skull.

Krall.

I'm going insane, she thought desperately. Case and point were when Logan reached for the knife, she jerked back, pulling it out of his reach.

No! The thought was instinctive, and her fingers tightened over the handle, echoing a sentiment that ran through her entire body. *Mine.*

"Easy." Logan took a step back. "I lost it. I just want it back, is all. I'm not going to hurt you, Serana."

She believed him. More than that, she *wanted* to give him his knife back. Until he *reached* for it again.

No. The thought was too loud, as if someone—or something—were bellowing inside her skull. *It's mine...*

"I-I don't think that's such a good idea, on second thought," she blurted, stumbling back until her shoulders hit the hard surface of a bookshelf, and there was plenty of space between them. "How do I know that it's even yours? You probably s-stole it."

Logan looked at her as if she'd grown a thousand heads. Better yet, he looked at her as if she was bat-shit crazy and needed to be locked up. Which wasn't much of a stretch since she was currently brandishing his own knife at him.

"Serana, look. I just want my knife back. I don't want to cause any trouble—just give it to me, and I'll go."

I just want my knife back. Something in his words made her flinch.

"Is that it, huh?" she spat scathingly, shocked by the venom in her tone. "Fuck me. Get me out of the way so that you could what? Go tearing through my house in search of your stupid knife, and what else, huh?"

Whoa. Where the hell had that come from? Her own anger shocked her. The pain, too. The thought of being used once again reopened old wounds in her soul.

She blamed the hurt for what she said next. "Is that all I was? A pity fuck? A way to make yourself feel better before trying to *rob* me—or are you just too much of a selfish bastard to not care?"

"Serana! Put the knife down."

"NO!" Her hand jerked as he took a step closer—though she certainly hadn't done it on purpose. "Logan, get the fuck out," she managed to gasp.

"Serana—"

"Get out!"

"Okay." He froze, hands held before him. "Okay. Just let me—"

His hand shot out, and everything seemed to move in slow motion. She saw his fingers move toward the blade. Felt her hand twitch in response. Saw the blade biting deep into the pad of his finger.

Saw the blood…

"Fuck!" Logan reared back, popping his finger in his mouth to staunch the bleeding.

The sight made Serana gasp, and the knife finally slipped from her grasp.

"Logan! I'm so sorry. I didn't mean—"

"It's alright." He didn't sound angry, but his stern expression made her throat go dry. For once, those emerald eyes weren't mocking or full of teasing mischief. They were dark and impassive, roving from her face, down to the knife at her feet, and back again. Whatever he saw, made his jaw clench with alarm.

"Serana, what happened to your hand?"

"W-what?" Confused, she glanced down. *Oh, that.* She'd almost forgotten cutting herself the other night. By now, the wound had deepened to a burgundy hue and traversed the width of her palm. Startling, yes, but a mere papercut shouldn't have been so shocking to him. "I…I cut myself."

But had it always been so deep? Strangely, she couldn't even feel any pain, either. Just a faint tingling sensation reminiscent of frostbite.

"With what?" Logan demanded.

She didn't need to answer. He was already eyeing the knife with a look that made her hair stand on end.

"Serana, I need to—"

"Please go," the plea released with a sob. To her horror, tears also began falling, dribbling down her chin. "Just go. Please. *Please…*"

"Alright."

She couldn't watch him leave—only the sound of his footsteps and the quiet thud of the front door clicking shut let her know when he finally did. Alone, she slowly slumped to the floor.

What in the hell had just happened? Something told her that it was more than just "jaded lover syndrome" that had her lashing out at the man with his own knife.

In fact, it was something about that exact blade in question. When he had reached for it… She couldn't describe the emotion that ran through her. Protectiveness, maybe?

She had wanted to *protect* it—from him. The blade she thought had a name.

Burying her face in her hands, she could only hope that Logan didn't go running to the police or get her locked away in a psych ward.

Just like her father in more ways than one…

Stop it. She shook her head, pulling herself to her feet while leaning against the bookshelf for balance. The knife still waited by her feet, glowing in the daylight coming from the window.

Master. The soft whisper sounded familiar. Like the same, ancient voice that had bellowed in her dreams and urged her fear against Logan.

Krall. The knife was fucking talking to her. Inside her head.

Master, it said. *I am yours.*

And that was when Serana ran from the room. She only went as far as the living room, wrenching the glass doors of the study shut behind her. There, she fished her cell phone from her purse and shakily punched the number to the clinic.

She felt cold all over—shock probably. She barely recognized the voice of whoever answered the phone and put her on hold when she asked for Mirabelle.

When the other woman finally answered, those cheery tones were like a gentle slap, snapping her out of the daze. "Hey, Serana! What's up?"

It didn't take a lot of effort to devise an excuse about being sick and staying home. Mirabelle believed the lie easily, even offering to bring her over some hot soup later.

Though, maybe it wasn't exactly a lie now that she thought about it. She *was* sick—had to be. Mentally unstable enough to threaten a man with his own knife after all but sleeping with him the night before.

A knife she could hear, even now.

Terrified, she went into the bathroom, pulled off Logan's clothes, turned the shower on blast, and curled in a ball in the very back corner as the heat slowly leeched into her skin.

Master, she heard inside her head, even above the roar of the water.

I am yours...

CHAPTER

EIGHTEEN

Damn it. Logan barged through the door of the pub, heading blindly for the kitchen. Every muscle in his body felt charged—electrified.

He could smash a fist into a wall and not even care. Like he could bake everything alive in fire and crush the world into a thousand smithereens. Hasten the earth's destruction with a snap of his fingers.

And just not give a shit.

Part of it was due to the pain lancing through the pad of his finger, feeding a dark lust he tried to shove to the back of his mind—overall, his poor mood resulted from desperation.

Maybe with a little terror thrown in.

He didn't even notice Marcus behind the bar counter, lying in wait—but he certainly felt the punch that glanced off his jaw next.

"Fuck!" The blow knocked him back against the wall, but he kept his balance. So, the man was a little angry about him disobeying a direct order when it came to Serana—especially if he saw her leaving the apartment wearing his sweatpants.

Still, his punishment would have to wait.

"Save it for later," he grumbled as the bigger man came for him again. Gingerly he cupped the side of his face and groaned. It, paired with the fresh nick on his finger from his own blade, had the front of his jeans tightening uncomfortably.

"I'm waiting for an explanation." Marcus watched him—a fist still raised.

"You and me both." Logan spit some blood onto the floor, making a mental note to mop it up later. "We've got a problem. It's about Serana…and Krall."

Slowly, Marcus lowered his fist. "What do you mean?"

What *did* he mean? Well, that Serana had freaked the fuck out the moment he'd tried taking it. Not out of greed, either. No, she seemed possessed. Had whatever fate the daemon hunters intended for Mirabelle been passed onto her?

"Krall," Logan managed to convey to Marcus, who flinched at the venom in his tone. "I went to Serana's to find it, but it shielded itself from me."

"Shielded itself?" Though his inflection barely changed, Marcus' skepticism was apparent in every word. "Are you sure it was even there?"

"The fuck it was!" Logan couldn't have reined in his anger even if he tried. Impulsively he curled a fist and punched the surface of a nearby dining table.

A hairline crack appeared down the middle of the thick wood, before the entire thing snapped in half.

"You'll need to work overtime to pay for that," Marcus muttered absentmindedly. "But keep talking."

"Oh, it was there, alright," Logan hissed. "Whenever I called to it, it ignored me, but when Serana held it…"

He broke off as he pictured how those gray eyes had widened as she held his blade—as if she'd been afraid of him for a moment.

"What?" Marcus sounded eerily calm as he pulled back a chair from the ruined table and perched his massive girth on the end of it. "What happened next?"

"She wouldn't let me fucking touch it, that's what. She *cut* me," he added, trailing his injured finger along his bottom lip. "But I don't even think she realized she was doing it. It was like…"

He couldn't think of a word crazy enough to describe it.

There was something else, though. A detail he couldn't admit, not even to Marcus. Whenever Serana had held Krall in her hands, he could sense the blade's energy then, flaring up around her like a defensive cocoon.

Krall wanted to keep him away from her, and that just took the damn cake. Was that what made him so angry? Was he jealous of his own knife? Was that even *possible?*

He was so wrapped up in the twisted thoughts Marcus had to shout to be heard.

"What do you mean she wouldn't let you touch it?" Rather than alarmed, his brother looked thoughtful, stroking the black stubble over his chin.

"What I said!" Logan hissed between his teeth, trying to keep himself from letting loose on another table. "She freaked whenever I came near her. I had to leave before she had a nervous breakdown."

The sight of her crying, confused and helpless, had done him in. In fact, part of him wanted nothing more than to race back there and cradle her in his arms so that she never looked that way again.

The mushy bullshit, he blamed on lack of sleep—the anger, however, was purely justified.

"Krall *ignored* me," he repeated. "Has your knife ever done that to you?"

"Ericur?" He didn't need to see Marcus' firm shake of his head to know that his brother had never experienced disobedience from his blade. He doubted any other daemon had—trust his luck to get a rebellious weapon.

The confusing nature of it all was enough to shatter any fear he might have had about coming clean. "There's something else you should know…"

With a sigh, he told Marcus everything from his stint in prison, to the white-haired daemon and, finally, his task to cut Mirabelle. Oddly enough, he couldn't tell what his brother thought about the betrayal. When he finished, Marcus just nodded.

"I knew you were hiding something," he admitted. "I assumed you intended to steal from me. Not this."

"I'm sorry," Logan said. "It was either play nice with a group of crazy hunters or prison—"

"I'm not angry," Marcus insisted, crossing his arms. "I would have been a fool to think you'd come out of the blue with no reason. Like I said, I have precautions in place. We wouldn't be having this conversation if your intentions were truly evil. But this does present a problem. Daemon hunters in Meyweather? I don't like the sound of that."

"If they even are daemon hunters," Logan countered. "The woman who recruited me was a full-blooded daemon. Silver hair. Bitchy personality. She didn't exactly seem like a white knight for the universe."

"When is the last time you saw them?"

He furrowed his brows, mulling it over. "When I got out of prison, there was a daemon who drove me to a portal site. Then I entered the mortal realm and laid low while I recovered. A few weeks later, I found a brochure in my hotel room advertising Meyweather. I didn't put it there. I guess they got impatient."

"So, you didn't rush here to do their bidding the second you were released?" Marcus asked.

Logan made a show of rolling his eyes. "No. I wasn't in a hurry to betray a Raeth daemon and take on the harbinger of the apocalypse. Sue me."

And if that little pointed reminder hadn't nudged him to act, he'd probably still be in Las Vegas, "recovering" with whatever woman he came across that day. As a result, he would have never met Mirabelle. Or Serana.

"And they haven't contacted you since?" Marcus asked, an eyebrow raised. "A group of daemon hunters spring you from prison and then patiently wait for you to uphold your end of the bargain?"

Logan frowned. "Well, when you put it that way…"

"It sounds like your mission might have been a decoy to lure you here in the first place. But why? Have you been followed?"

Logan shrugged. "There was this creepy ass bird, but I'm not sure."

"Well," Marcus continued, "there is one person who would know whether your friends were legitimate or not, but first? We need to find out what might be happening to Serana. Wait here."

He stood and padded over to the pay phone he kept against the back wall. After punching in a code that overrode the pay system, Marcus dialed a number and waited.

The figure on the other end must have answered on the first ring, because not even a second later, Marcus grumbled through what had to be one of the shortest, oddest conversations Logan had heard in his life.

"I need an appointment," Marcus began. There was a brief pause as he waited for the other person to respond. "Now, preferably," he replied. "Daemon business."

There was another pause, shorter than the last, as if this was a well-rehearsed conversation as played-out as a script.

"We'll be there within the hour," Marcus said after a moment.

With that, he hung up and paused to grab a jacket from one of the hooks along the wall before heading for the door.

"The person we need to see lives on the edge of town, so we need to go now—" He turned, and Logan had only a split-second's warning to catch a pair of keys flung in his direction. "You drive."

"Wait… Was that Jace? He agreed to come here just like that?"

"Jace? No." Marcus raised an eyebrow. "I'll contact him later. This is about your knife."

Logan hated the feeling of hesitation that had him lingering on the threshold of the pub, keys in hand. "What about Serana?"

It didn't feel right to leave her alone. Not terrified of him… or maybe it was herself?

Whoever Marcus was taking him to see didn't seem worth the risk of what she might do trapped in that damn house all by herself.

Marcus shrugged, nodding to the pocket where Logan kept his cell phone.

"Call someone to keep an eye on her."

Logan raised a skeptical eyebrow. "Who?"

All it took was one knowing look from Marcus for a name to pop into his mind.

Mirabelle.

He almost couldn't dial her number quick enough, and when she answered, he made up some lie of being concerned for Serana after watching her throw up last night after everyone had left.

Not very tactful, but hey. The lie piqued Mirabelle's concern enough that Logan knew she wouldn't let Serana out of her sight.

Only then, did he follow Marcus to his truck and climb into the driver's seat. He didn't waste his breath asking questions about where they were going or who they were supposed to see.

NINETEEN

Serana felt sane enough after a long shower to get dressed and proceed to the kitchen. It was only then, while cradling a mug of fresh coffee, that she could dissect what had happened with Logan.

I cut him, again, she mentally acknowledged. *I have got to stop doing that.*

It wasn't like she wanted to hurt him—*that* time anyway. One potential explanation made her heart lurch. *Krall did it.* In the moment, she hadn't been in control—the knife had…

Which was downright silly. Either she was blaming an inanimate object for her own impulsive violence, or the thing had a will of its own.

And a name.

Ultimately, she didn't know exactly what made her return to the study. Morbid curiosity?

Unsurprisingly, the knife was still there. Cautiously, she grabbed her discarded nightshirt and wrapped the cotton around her hand. Then she picked up the blade like one would a squished spider.

With her bundle in hand, she entered the kitchen and placed it on the table, as far away from her seat as physically possible.

Funnily enough, it didn't look *evil*. There was something mesmerizing about the dark, twisted designs over the blade. Slowly, she pushed her mug aside and trailed the tip of her finger along the sharp edge.

Master.

She gasped and jerked back so hard her chair squeaked. Still, she forced herself to stay seated. Feeling very much like an idiot, she purposefully stroked the blade again, and a guttural voice bellowed inside her skull, *Master.* She noted the tone was softer this time, as if…whatever it was, was trying hard not to scare her.

Voice shaking, she attempted to answer it. "K-Krall?"

Yes. A burst of warmth jolted through her fingers. *Master.*

"M-Master?" Serana had to lick her lips just to find the strength to keep going. "W-what do you mean by…"

She couldn't even bring herself to say that word out loud again. It felt way too weird. Almost as weird as talking to a knife.

You are my master, Krall said simply. *I am yours to command.*

Command? "But…but you're *Logan's* knife." Serana felt the need to stress that part. *Logan, whom you made me cut.*

Logan is my caller, the blade replied gently, as if talking to a frightened child. You *are my master. I am yours to command.*

Oh, to hell with it, Serana thought tiredly. If she was going insane, why not plunge in headfirst?

"Command to do what?" she asked.

Images filled her head in response. Bloody, violent images—none of them pleasant. When she shuddered in disgust, they faded away, and a soft whisper replaced them, *whatever you desire. I am yours to command.*

"Did you—" She broke off, making her voice a little stronger. "Why did you make me attack Logan—especially if he's your caller?"

Krall's response was firmer. Almost…angry. *You were frightened,* it explained. *Krall will harm even his caller to protect you.*

Serana shook her head. "I wasn't—"

Afraid. But that was a lie. Logan absolutely terrified her—but not because he might hurt her. Deep down, the truth was far more pathetic—she was afraid of wanting him. Of wanting him too much to back down against the boundaries of casual sex. Hell, the guy was a stranger, but a part of her actually wanted to know him more.

Krall does not make distinctions between fear, the blade said defensively, as if reading her thoughts. *You were threatened, so Krall reacted—as I will* always *react to protect you.*

The vehement promise made her withdraw her hand.

"What do you think I need protection from?"

There was a slight pause. Almost as if the knife were using its judgment to avoid giving her an answer. In the end, the same gravely uttered words echoed in her mind.

I will always protect you.

A daunting vow considering that its owner only seemed to be interested in one-night stands. Speaking of said playboy…

"Can Logan talk to you, like I can?"

No. She pictured the knife shaking its head, if it had one. *Logan does not bother to speak to Krall. Therefore, Krall does not bother to speak to him.*

Fair enough, but the words brought up another valid point.

"Why me?" she demanded, almost in a whisper. "Why can you talk to me?"

Because you are my master—my beholder. I am bound to you, therefore I am sworn to serve—

"B-Bound to me?"

An affirmative burn shot through her fingertips.

Always. From now until the end of time.

"B-but how?" she pressed. "Why? Why me?"

You are my master. Krall sounded softer, as if this conversation had exhausted its desire to talk. *I am bound to serve, as you wish. So is my caller. We are yours...*

Serana opened her mouth, ready to ask something else, when a sudden knock on the door made her lunge to her feet. Without thinking, she snatched Krall from the table and shoved it in the nearest drawer.

I have waited for my beholder for countless years, the blade whispered as it landed among a bunch of old cookie cutters. *I am yours to command.*

The words haunted her as she darted into the hallway and wrenched open the front door before the figure on the other end could knock again.

"Hi!"

The sight of Mirabelle, standing in the doorway like a golden ray of sunshine, startled Serana so badly she took a step back.

"What are you doing here?"

"Serana, you look..." Mirabelle's smile slipped, only to be replace by a worried frown. "Horrible," she exclaimed before shoving her way into the foyer. In one hand, she held a bag of groceries. "I should have realized how bad off you were just from how horrible you sounded on the phone." Still speaking, she headed into the kitchen, leaving Serana no choice but to follow. "But when Logan called and told me about last night, I knew that I had to come over—"

"Last night?" If Mirabelle hadn't reached out to place a steadying hand on her shoulder, she might have fallen over. "What did Logan tell you about last night?"

Mirabelle nodded sympathetically. "About how you got sick after everyone left. It's probably just a 24-hour bug. Don't worry though, this—" She hefted her bulging grocery bag, "will fix you right up."

Serana eyed the plastic skeptically. "And just what is that?"

"Canned soup, Sprite, and beer." Mirabelle ticked off each item on the fingers of her free hand. "Sure to fix you right up."

As exhausted, confused, and borderline insane as Serana felt, she couldn't resist croaking a weak laugh. "Beer?"

Mirabelle winked. "Family secret. Now you go and rest while I make this up for you. Shoo!"

For once, Serana didn't feel the urge to fight. It felt good to have Mirabelle there—someone who had a mouth to talk back. She only paused near the doorway of the living room to ask, "What about work?"

"On my lunch break," Mirabelle chirped in reply. "Now *rest.*"

It wasn't very reluctantly that Serana padded into the living room and sank against the cushions of the couch. She felt guilty having Mirabelle wait on her, but for once, that guilt was overwhelmed by fear.

I've been alone too long, she thought, resting against the pillows. Way too long if she had taken to chatting up knives for company.

Still, as her eyes slid shut, she couldn't help but dwell on something Mirabelle had said.

When *Logan* called. Obviously, he wasn't mad at her— though sending Mirabelle could be his method of revenge?

As her mind drifted off, she couldn't help but wonder...

Logan was surprised when Marcus decided to reward his patience about twenty minutes into the drive by revealing some breadcrumbs of information. He had been silent until then, muttering only the occasional direction.

Damn Raeths and their secrecy. Not that Logan made a habit of befriending many daemons of that race or otherwise. Marcus served as his first venture into a somewhat close, kind of friendly relationship with anyone, and he wasn't sure yet if he enjoyed the comradery.

"We're on our way to see a witch I know," his brother said. "She's young, and not very experienced, but she knows way more about daemonic weapons than I do. Be patient with her, and I'm sure we'll learn something useful."

"Young," Logan replied. "That means she isn't our dear, old mother, at least."

Though, he could admit that the thick, emerald forest lining the edge of the road wasn't Liva's vibe. Neither were small mortal towns in the middle of nowhere.

"Of course not," Marcus replied. "She is… I'll explain when we get there. We're not far."

Logan envied his brother's calm. All he could think about was Serana. He barely heard Marcus speak, until the man shouted his name.

"Huh?" Logan snapped back to awareness, swerving to miss a dip in the road.

Marcus deliberately adjusted his seat belt. "I said my *friend,* the one we're going to see, will be able to tell us what's going on with Krall. If it's daemon related, at least. Though, she won't be able to help us with your Protectors of the Dawn. We'll deal with that later once we have a better idea of what you've gotten yourself into."

Logan scoffed. "I know what's going on," he muttered darkly as Marcus gestured for him to take the next turn. "Those daemon hunting sons of bitches did something to it. Whatever is happening to Serana was *meant* to happen to Mirabelle. You should have called Jace," he added, referring to their MIA, daemon hunter of a brother. "He would know more than some witch."

"Maybe." A slight inflection in Marcus' tone made Logan hold his tongue. "Though, he might question why you made a deal with supposed hunters in the first place. Krall is your responsibility. You know better than to let it out of your sight. Instead of chasing ass, you should have been watching your back—"

"I know that, okay?" Logan snapped. The last thing he needed was a lecture from *Mr. Holier Than Thou* to rub it in that he was a piece of shit. "Let's hope this witch, or whatever, can help me fix it."

Without him risking another injury.

"She should," Marcus replied with confidence Logan didn't feel himself. "The key will be to be polite. Do things on her terms and try to rein in your more...impulsive Shael instincts. Patience is key."

A moment later, the road turned into a grove of ash trees— at the edge of which, waited a small red house on a gray foundation of stone. All in all, it resembled a summer cabin rather than a witch's hut.

At Marcus' direction, Logan parked beside a small shed and followed his brother over to the dwelling. Before they could knock, a slender figure appeared behind a screen door.

"Marcus!" she chirped. "Come in! Come in!"

Logan didn't know what he'd expected. Definitely not this bouncing ball of blond fluff.

"Hazel." Marcus greeted her with a respectful nod and attempted to shake her hand. The woman—or perhaps, young girl?—pulled him into a hug instead.

"I told you not to be a stranger!" She giggled, playfully slapping him on the shoulder. "Now, what is this about a daemon blade?"

Logan skeptically glanced her over. This, *Hazel*, looked hardly big enough to even hold a blade, let alone know about daemonic forms of the weapon. She barely came to his shoulder —shorter than even Serana. Cropped blond hair framed a pale face crowned by two massive brown eyes. He guessed that she was sixteen. *Maybe*, with a few years to go before he'd feel comfortable with the loving way she eyed Marcus.

"How about we have a seat first?" Marcus suggested.

"Sure." The girl led the way into a small living room that smelled faintly of incense. While Logan wasn't versed much in the history of this country—the mortal version anyway —he'd read some books. Enough to suspect the décor looked like something ripped from a Native American museum, with woven blankets tossed over nearly every surface and delicate beadwork hanging on the walls.

Logan also suspected that Hazel didn't appear to have so much as a drop of said blood running through her veins— though, looks could be deceiving. After all, he and Marcus didn't exactly *look* part daemon.

"I just put some tea on," Hazel chirped. "You're welcome to have some!"

Biting his tongue against a nasty retort, Logan sat on the end of a wooden bench while Marcus took the seat across from him.

"I would love some tea," his brother said warmly.

Beaming, Hazel rushed off to pour him a cup. When she returned, armed with a pink mug speckled with teddy bears, the man unashamedly took a deep sip.

"Tell her," he prompted after another sip, nodding at Logan.

Gritting his teeth, Logan tried to ignore the fact he was requesting advice from little more than a teenager as he retold the incident with Serana and his blade. As he spoke, that childish gleam left Hazel's gaze.

She waited until he finished before sitting back in her chair, clasping her pale hands, brightened by pink nails.

"*Daemonic el Moria,*" she breathed softly.

While he didn't understand them, the words sent a shiver down Logan's spine. "What does it mean?"

"Master of the blade," Hazel explained, a note of awe in her voice. "It's old lore—ancient. Something I only found mentioned in my grandmother's old notes—a beholder of the blade—"

"I'm the 'beholder' of Krall," Logan interrupted, thinking of the day—when he had been five years old—his mother stabbed him in the chest with it. He'd had it ever since. "It belongs to me."

"You are the weapon's caller," Hazel corrected, rolling her eyes. "It is bound to you, entwined in your life force, but you are not its *beholder,* the wielder. The person whom you and your blade are bound to serve."

"Bound to… What the hell do you—"

"Logan," Marcus warned, still holding his pink mug. "Just listen to her. Go on, Hazel."

"The beholder," she continued, raising her voice. "Is the wielder of the blade. The one to whom it has marked with innocent blood—"

"Holy shit," Logan's voice broke as he pictured the scar on Serana's palm. "She must have cut herself on it."

"It tasted her blood and decided to choose her," Hazel suspected with a knowing nod. "That's that. She is bound to you and you to her."

"The fuck?" was all Logan could croak in response.

"What does this mean?" Marcus asked before taking another sip of his tea. "What does being the beholder entail?"

"Fealty," Hazel said with another dreamy smile. "This woman is the only one capable of controlling the blade and unleashing its true power. With it, she can either protect or destroy you."

Destroy, Logan thought with a pinch of unease. Especially if her reaction this morning was an indicator of anything.

But that wasn't the sole worry weighing on his mind.

"But wait. What if... Let's say Krall 'tasted' someone else's blood first," he said. "Like say...another daemon. Or half daemon?"

The harbinger of doom, for instance.

"An interesting question." Hazel wrinkled her nose and shrugged. "I think the race doesn't matter. Just if they are of innocent blood. Though, I would assume the blade has discretion in who it chooses. For the sake of conversation, let's say they would probably have become your beholder instead."

Ice ran down Logan's spine. If he'd cut Mirabelle first, she would potentially be the "beholder" of the blade. As far as he knew, Mirabelle seemed to be the only known child of Liva without a daemonic weapon. Why would so-called daemon hunters want to arm the harbinger of doom with one as powerful as Krall?

He couldn't think of a good reason, himself. Warily, he eyed Marcus. Judging from his stern frown, his brother was thinking along the same lines.

"Fealty," Marcus repeated. "Does that mean Logan will be subservient to this woman?"

Logan couldn't hide his disgust. "The hell I will!"

"In a sense," Hazel said over him. "He will be driven to protect her at any cost. It's fate. He won't be able to resist the instinct."

"How do I fix it?" Logan asked. "This woman is mortal. She doesn't understand—"

"You can't 'fix' it," Hazel snapped, sounding like a teenager again. "The blade has chosen her. She is the beholder of your weapon, whether you like it or not. Though," she added on a sniff, "her being mortal simplifies things. If you truly wanted to get rid of her, I suppose you could just let her die."

"What?" Logan felt his brows furrow. "What do you mean let her die? Answer me, you little—"

"You're really rude." Hazel watched him with an unreadable expression. Then, with a gulp, she drained her mug and set it down. "It was nice seeing you, Marcus," she said pleasantly. "Do visit me again, some time? *Alone*. Promise?"

"Will do," Marcus said with a respectful nod. To Logan's annoyance, the man just stood as if the girl hadn't said something monumental.

"Wait—what the hell did you mean by die—"

"Logan." Marcus' tone was sharp as he inclined his head toward the door. "It's time to go." To Hazel, he flashed one of his lopsided smiles and ruffled that blond hair again. "Tell your grandmother I said hello the next time you see her."

"Sure thing," Hazel promised, gazing at him with puppy dog eyes. "She misses you almost as much as I do."

Logan was still grappling with the thought that Serana could die if he didn't...what? He was tempted to wrap his hands around that pale throat and demand some answers—

but he wasn't stupid. Marcus wasn't the type to tiptoe around anyone.

Not without a damn good reason.

Reluctantly, Logan stood and followed the two to the door. There, Hazel turned to him.

"*You*," she said, facing him with her hands on her hips. "Seek me out again when you learn some manners, and I will tell you what is needed to keep the mortal woman safe. Until then…"

She flounced off, allowing the screen door to slam shut behind her.

Logan watched her fade into the shadows of the house with a growl. "That little—"

"Hush," Marcus was already waiting by the truck. "You got the answers you wanted, didn't you? *Some* of them, anyway. Bide your time, and you'll learn more soon enough."

"Yeah," Logan spat scathingly, as he climbed into the driver's seat and palmed the steering wheel. "I got every-thing but the main part of it—you know that little detail where Serana could die if I don't…do something. Isn't she under your protection? You should give a damn what happens to her!"

"I do," Marcus replied with genuine concern in his voice. "This isn't good."

"No," Logan agreed. In fact, he was tempted to tell Marcus to go to Hell and march back into that house to demand that little bitch tell him the truth.

"Who is she, anyway?" he demanded, shoving the key in the ignition. "A little young for you, if you ask me. And with a smart-ass mouth for a kid."

Marcus sighed before responding. "She is our youngest sister."

He didn't give Logan the chance to process that bombshell before adding, "And while her fate isn't as devastating as Mirabelle's, she is more dangerous than you can imagine. I suggest you tread carefully around her, unless you like being burned alive by hellfire."

Logan gulped. That was an old, powerful magic he'd only heard of through rumors. "Like mother like daughter."

"No." Marcus shook his head. "She is nothing like Liva. Neither do I think she is part of the children foreseen in the prophecy, because she isn't part daemon but a full witch."

Which meant that Liva had at least eight children running around—a chilling prospect.

"Even so," Marcus continued, "she has no idea what she's capable of, and it needs to stay that way. Frankly, I didn't think you were ready to meet her. Given the circumstances, I made an exception. Don't make me regret that."

"You're more worried than you let on," Logan realized. "About Serana and Krall. Admit it. What the hell aren't you saying?"

Marcus met his gaze without a hint of guilt. "Logan, I think your mishap with Serana may have prevented the end of the world. For now, anyway. If she dies, and the initial plan of your 'friends' comes to fruition, who knows what will happen as a result. So yes, consider me worried."

Logan didn't know what to say. Hearing Marcus' concerns out loud cemented just how badly he'd fucked up—and how much was still at stake.

"What should I do?"

"Wait for Hazel's call," Marcus suggested. "And don't let Serana Blake out of your sight. From now on, consider her your primary focus. If anything happens to her, I will hold you responsible. Apocalypse or not, you will suffer. I'll see to it personally."

TWENTY-ONE

The living room was drenched in shadow when Serana awoke. She had slept twice that day, the most she had in months, yet she felt exhausted. It took everything she had just to pull herself upright. As she placed her feet on the floor, she caught sight of a note someone had left on the coffee table.

Serana, I didn't want to wake you, so I left the soup in the microwave and the beer and soda in the fridge. Get well soon! —that bit had been punctuated with a neatly drawn smiley face. *P.S. DO NOT HESITATE TO CALL ME—Mirabelle.*

Serana didn't know whether to be flattered by the woman's concern or annoyed. Not even a second later, she heard a knock on the door.

"Mirabelle." She tried to keep the irritation from her voice as she headed for the door and opened it. "Thank you, but I'm fine—really."

As soon as she saw who waited on the other side, the words died in her throat.

"Hello," the woman said with a wary smile.

As stunning as Mirabelle, she had blond hair, large brown eyes, and skin that was peachy cream. She might have even been just as kind as Mirabelle—though Serana couldn't be sure, seeing as how it had been almost twelve years since she'd last seen the woman in front of her.

"Hello, Serana," Zoe repeated in a wavering voice. "Were you expecting someone else?"

Serana shook her head, too stunned to speak. It was like seeing a ghost after all these years. A living, breathing shadow of her past.

"May I come in?"

Numb, Serana stood back, allowing the woman she'd once loved like a sister to enter her home. She even smelled the same, like honey and roses and crisp perfume.

"It's been a while…" With a nervous laugh, Zoe glanced around the foyer, twirling a piece of white-blond hair around her finger. "Being in this town brings back so many memories."

She sounded pleased at that—as if her only thoughts of this town and house had been bright, pleasant, and brimming with joy.

Nothing like Serana's. Zoe didn't live in fear of the ice that threatened to swallow her. She didn't have to suffer in the shadows of this house and try not to…

Suffocate.

No, Serana thought, taking the woman in with a broad sweep from head to toe. Zoe didn't look like she'd spent the last few years in a world of ice.

"Can we sit down?" the woman asked, after a long, awkward moment of standing in the foyer.

Serana hesitated. She wasn't exactly being a good host, but who the hell would be, given the circumstances? Something in her gut warned that whatever had brought Zoe back to Meyweather, could not be good—for her.

"Sure," she said, turning to lead the way back into the living room, which now felt as comfortable as walking over shards of glass. She forced herself to take a seat. Forced herself to keep her face blank and her mouth shut, when all she really wanted to do was demand that Zoe tell her what the hell she wanted and leave.

With her fake smile firmly in place, Zoe took a seat as well —the velvet chaise, which was the spot furthest from her one could be without standing. Only then, did the edges of her mouth fall, leaving a wary expression that promised a shit-ton of bad news.

"Serana," Zoe began in a tight voice. "We need to talk."

She opened her mouth…

And Serana bolted upright, moving into the kitchen with a watery sigh. "Can I get you anything to drink?" she called, but by then, she was already rummaging through the fridge, drawing out one of the beers Mirabelle had left inside without shame and reaching for a coffee mug.

"Ah…water would be nice?" Zoe seemed to choke out.

Water? *Good,* Serana thought through gritted teeth as she pulled out a glass and filled it with water from the tap. Then, she poured her beer into a mug and brought both back into the living room—too shaken up to feel ashamed that she needed a buzz to face her stepsister.

She handed Zoe her glass, and took a deep sip from her mug before sitting back down, steeling herself against whatever the woman might say. She didn't give the go-ahead to speak, but, with a sigh, Zoe did anyway.

"Serana, I know you probably don't want to see me—trust me," she said, taking a sip of her own water before continuing, "it took a lot out of me, just to show up. But we *need* to talk. It's about this house and…your father's will."

No. Serana squeezed her eyes shut, gulping beer like crazy until the harsh burn was enough to counter whatever pinch in her chest Zoe's words might inspire.

She was Serana Blake—or so she tried to tell herself. Cool, calm, and collected. Nothing Zoe could say about her father could surprise her more than the other dark truths she'd learned about in the months since his death.

Ha, something in her cackled. *The fuck it can't.*

"What?" she croaked, hating how damn tired she sounded. "Just cut to the chase, Zoe—why the hell are you here?"

If Zoe were surprised at all by the venom in her tone, she didn't show it. All the woman did was run a hand through her long blond hair and sigh—Serana figured it was only practice in sensing out weakness that made her notice the way the woman's hand trembled.

"It's about the house, Serana," Zoe said on another shaky exhale of air. "In his will…William left part of it to me."

Part of it…

Which Serana figured was just about the whole damn thing. Despite her mental warnings to herself, she felt shock run through her like a lance. Sinking deep, tearing open old wounds.

As if from far away, she heard the tinkling smash of her mug hitting the floor, spilling beer all down the front of her sweatshirt. Zoe looked as if she'd expected the reaction and still felt nothing but pity.

But Serana didn't care.

She just didn't fucking care.

"Get out." Serana didn't even recognize the voice that tore from her throat, as guttural as Logan's had been after she'd cut him. Without glancing at Zoe, she stood and headed for the door. "You need to leave."

"Serana…" Zoe's plea was half-hearted, as if she had fully expected this reaction and wasn't surprised. "It's in his will

—I tried to have the lawyers call you, but you never returned any of our—"

The lawyers call her. Which meant that, if Zoe had her way, she wouldn't have had to show up at all. Tell her to her face that her own father had loved another man's daughter more than his own. Enough to leave to her, in his will, the one and only thing that Serana should have been given by right.

It was almost too funny. Serana laughed—just a sharp bark, punctuated by so much pain she couldn't stand it.

Fuck it. She whirled around on her heel, turning to face Zoe in the narrow confines of the hallway—loving the way those soft brown eyes widened ever so slightly, as if the woman was afraid she might hit her or something.

As if she'd give the bitch the satisfaction of filing a lawsuit against her.

"Serana," she said, sounding a little more desperate this time. "Trust me, I didn't want you to find out like this. I wanted to—"

"Find out what?" Serana spat, hating the tears that burned behind her eyes. *No,* she snarled mentally, shoving them back. *Not now.*

At Zoe, she narrowed her eyes, until she knew they were the frosty slits they both knew so well.

"Find out that my father left the one thing in the world that should belong to *me*, to a selfish bitch who couldn't even bother to show up to his funeral? Ha!" Another harsh laugh, though this time it sounded decidedly broken. "Spare me the false dramatics, Zoe—now get the fuck out."

The woman's eyes widened, but that pert mouth tightened, more determinedly than ever.

"Serana." Her voice was soothing soft, and so much like Mirabelle's that she found herself listening despite herself. "The house is yours. He left you—"

"Shut up," Serana snarled, so icily the sound made her own skin crawl. "Don't you dare talk about my father like you knew him."

As horrible as he was, even Zoe didn't deserve that right.

"You come halfway across the country only now to tell me this? You should have told me at the damn *funeral*, Zoe— you should have been there!" The pain in her voice surprised her.

Wait, was *that* why she was upset? Not because the girl had left all those years ago and never come back, but because…

"You let me go through that by myself," she went on, ignoring the dangerous edge on which her voice wavered, threatening to crack. And what was that harsh gasp? Yep, that definitely sounded like the beginnings of a sob—but once she'd started on this little tirade, she was surprised to find that she couldn't stop. "You should have been there for *me*—I had no one!"

She could barely see Zoe's face now. Just a blur through tears she hadn't even realized had started to fall. Angrily, she reached up to wipe them away with the back of her hand, glad she couldn't see Zoe's face as she uttered a quiet reply.

"I know."

It was that quiet little acknowledgment of her own heart-wrenching pain that sent Serana over the edge.

Without another word, she marched to the door and yanked it open to reveal a darkly silent street. "Get out," she croaked, jabbing a finger through the doorway.

She waited until Zoe slipped by her with another sigh. Until the woman moved elegantly onto the porch and spun to face her. Those pink lips parted, probably for one last apology…

And Serana slammed the door in her face.

Then she slumped, heart pounding, to the floor with her back resting against the solid wood and just…came apart.

She screamed wordlessly.

Rocked herself back and forth with her face buried in her hands—but nothing worked. Nothing she did, screamed, or shouted could make that burning, stabbing pain disappear. It was almost on a desperate burst of energy that she lurched to her feet and smashed a fist against the face of the old grandfather clock that had ticked faithfully away by the staircase for as long as she could remember.

Beneath her fist, the glass spider-webbed and cracked, but it wasn't until she braced both hands on one side of the thing and pushed with all her might that it fell to the floor and smashed into huge chunks of splintered wood and glass.

Feel better? a part of her coldly remarked. The rage running through her was about as foreign as the way Zoe had seemed to her after all this time—but she had a feeling that it had been just slumbering inside her.

With her unannounced visit, Zoe had woken a sleeping giant, and it was fucking pissed.

Serana moved like a woman with a mission through the house, swiping old figurines and knick-knacks from the shelves as she marched up the stairs and threw open the door to her room. She packed without any semblance of common sense—just threw stuff into an old duffle bag and hefted it over her shoulder.

Then, she made off for her father's room—the one place in the house she hadn't brought herself to venture into until then. It was as stuffy as he had been, and seemed a couple degrees colder than even the rest of the house did.

A tomb of ice.

She didn't break anything in there. All she did, was move carefully into the closet, near the very back, where she found a box of old hunting gear. Inside she found something that looked like a sheath, strapped to a belt, a box of matches, and a military-issue flashlight.

The sheath, she strapped around her waist, over her jeans, before shoving everything else into her duffle. Then, she grabbed some money from the safe she knew the bastard kept locked behind a portrait of a winter landscape above his dresser and returned downstairs before old memories could steal her nerve.

Regardless, she could still hear his voice in her head, hissing that she'd never be anything like Zoe.

A girl who wasn't even his.

She had to reach up to swipe more tears away by the time she stumbled into the kitchen. Her impulse was to grab more beer, but even she knew better. Instead, she fished a box of crackers, a bottle of water from the fridge, and two cans of the soup Mirabelle had brought. She shoved those into her duffle, before pausing to grab Logan's knife from the cookie-cutter drawer and tucking the blade carefully into the sheath at her waist.

You are upset, it seemed to hum with concern as her shaky fingers clutched the hilt. *You sense danger.*

That was an understatement. The entire house repelled her, disgusted her, terrified her. She couldn't spend another night here, alone.

If she did, then she knew she'd really go insane…

She couldn't bring herself to answer Krall as she drew her sweater down over the sheath. Instead, she hefted her duffle over her shoulder and moved into the garage before the icy, suffocating cold made her physically sick.

She had to fight down a gag or two as she climbed into her car—the only thing in this place that was truly hers, bought and paid for by her own money—and peeled out of there like a bat out of Hell.

She had only a vague idea of where she was going—some old cabin near the mountains her father used when he hunted. The maps were somewhere in her glove compartment. She'd always planned on going there to see if there was anything in there that could be used to pay off the man's estate.

Now, certainly didn't seem like a good time to go traipsing around the woods without a clue of where she was going—but what other choice did she have?

She wouldn't last another minute in that house.

Somehow, she managed to make it halfway out of town—right near the old bridge by the Windon farm—when a dark shape ran out into the middle of the road. Panicked, she swerved to avoid it, but the car jumped off the shoulder.

And crashed.

TWENTY-TWO

Logan drove aimlessly as Marcus' warning echoed in his mind. He was tempted to scoff at the concept. Krall cutting Serana wasn't the end of the world—literally.

However, the hellish imagery conveyed by his nightmares haunted him. What if Maribelle wasn't the harbinger after all…

Or he was being a superstitious fool. Besides, it didn't matter what some teenage witch claimed. Nothing bad would happen. To *Serana,* anyway.

Sooner or later, the daemon hunters would come calling for *him.* If they were feeling charitable, they'd merely drag him back to Arcaneum. If not, it wouldn't matter if Mirabelle triggered an apocalypse. He'd be dead by then.

A smart man would leave town and take his chances blending into the mortal plane. Though realistically, he couldn't hide for long, only prolong the inevitable.

Then what?

His plan didn't stretch that far. For what felt like hours, he just navigated the roads of Meyweather until a familiar house came into view, and, just like that, Serana Blake returned to the forefront of his mind.

Marcus had given him his blessing and—even if he didn't believe in the teenage witch's spiel—why not take advantage of his directive to keep an eye on her.

Oddly enough, her car wasn't in the open garage. Strange. He kept driving, heading through town with no clear direction in mind.

When his phone rang, he assumed it was Marcus calling for a status update. The trembling voice that answered him, however, quashed that theory.

"Serana?" he asked.

"I…I need your help."

Logan's blood ran cold at the pain lacing her tone. "What's wrong?" He couldn't have kept the panic from his voice if he had tried. "Serana? Damn it!"

The line went dead, but it was as if a part of him already knew where to go. As he neared an old bridge on the outskirts of Meyweather, an ominous sense of dread knotted in his gut. Then he saw it—a familiar black car yards from the road, pitched at an awkward angle.

"Serana!" He lunged from his truck and raced to the vehicle, more alarmed the closer he came—it was stuck in a ditch, one wrong move from overturning completely. Frantic, he peered through the windshield and nearly howled with relief when the lone occupant groggily turned to face him.

She looked like shit.

Her eyes were bloodshot, and a nasty bruise snaked along her jaw. The fact that she was moving made him sigh in relief as he raced to the driver's side door and wrenched it open.

"Logan." Her voice was low, resonating with a deep-seated emotion that had him pulling her closer before she'd even found her footing. "I'm sor—"

He cut her off with a curse smothered into her hair as he eyed the wreckage.

A nicely-sized dent shaped the front bumper, and broken glass littered the ground. The damage was minimal—nothing that couldn't be repaired with a week in the shop. Serana looked worse, though. Much worse.

She winced as he tilted her face gingerly with his thumb.

"What the hell happened?" he asked, though it was a struggle to keep from shouting.

"I'm fine. I..." Serana sighed. "There was a bird in the road. I swerved—"

"A bird?" He whirled around but found nothing else in view. Still, a part of him tightened with unease. So much for the hunters coming after him. What if they decided to erase his mistake first?

"It was huge," Serana muttered, drawing his focus back to her. "A crow or something, I didn't—"

Suddenly, Logan frowned as he sensed a sharp, acidic smell wafting off her. One he knew all too well.

"Fuck, were you drinking?"

She shook her head, but her eyes were bloodshot. She swayed on her feet, and despite the slightly warm night air, she was shivering.

Daemon knife or not, any doubts he felt toward their strange arrangement vanished. "I'm taking you to the hospital." Before she could argue, he turned for his truck, pulling her after him.

"No." The soft hitch in her voice shocked him—almost as much as the tears glistening in those gray eyes did. "No… I'm not drunk."

But something was wrong. The next second, Logan had her in his arms. The sight of her dazed and broken awoke something inside of him. Something fiercely protective that wanted to beat the living hell out of who or what was responsible for driving her out in the middle of the night. For the time being, he settled for asking, "What the hell happened?"

She said nothing, choosing to bury her face in his shirt instead. A moment later, he heard the harsh sounds of sobs.

"Serana." Helpless, he stroked her back, hoping she wasn't more severely injured than she looked. Glancing up the road, he shuddered. She wasn't far from a narrow bridge. If she'd been on it when she swerved…

The sobering thought made him crush her body to his chest, relishing the slight feel of her. As the seconds ticked past, he expected her to pull away. Shrug him off. Try to keep that icy cool, even broken and bloodied.

So he decided to beat her to the punch. "Let me take you to the hospital."

"No." She shook her head, smearing warm tears into the cotton of his shirt. "I'm *fine*."

Logan didn't even waste his breath pointing out the many ways she was *not* fine. All he did was gingerly trail a finger along the line of her jaw.

"You're bleeding," he said, trying to sound as reasonable as Marcus. "You could have a concussion."

And daemon hunters could be on her trail, aiming to do who knew what.

She shook her head, but as yellow headlights appeared in the distance, he suspected he needed to take her somewhere before a curious passerby decided to take matters into their own hands.

"If not to the hospital, then let me take you home—"

"No! I can't…I can't go home."

The pain in her tone made him stiffen. Had someone hurt her? At the thought, anger flared through him so swiftly. The fact that he still held her was the only thing keeping him from jumping back in his truck and peeling over to her house for answers.

In fact, screw the truck. It would only slow him down—he was much faster on foot.

But leaving her alone in this state wouldn't do much good if the Protectors of Dawn were truly after her.

Pushing aside his concern, for now, he carried her to his truck. She didn't fight as he eased her onto the passenger's seat, but when he loped around to the driver's side, he found her cradled against the door, face in her hands.

"If you won't let me take you home, then where were you going?"

She pulled back slightly from her hands to whisper, "Cabin. My father stayed there…when he hunted."

"You were going *alone*?" He couldn't keep a bit of bitterness from leaking into his tone at that.

Logan didn't know whether to shake or…kiss her as she glanced up at him, gray eyes huge in the light of the rising moon. He settled for gripping the steering wheel instead.

"Where?"

Serana shrugged. "I had a map…"

"Wait here." He returned to her car and tore through the glove compartment until he found a small brochure of the surrounding countryside. A duffle bag rested on the passenger's seat. Obviously, she'd been planning to spend a few days wherever she'd been trying to go.

Carrying both items, he reentered his truck and eyed Serana with a skeptical frown. She scared the hell out of him. Never had anyone made him feel this way—on edge. Like a dancer balancing on a fucking tight rope—one wrong move, and he'd fall.

More and more, the hospital seemed like the better option for her. In the end, he merely asked, "Tell me where to go."

"The cabin, I think. But my car," Serana croaked. "I can't just leave it—"

"Don't worry about it. I'll call someone."

Someone who just so happened to be Marcus. He'd end up owing the man even more for a favor like this, but Logan couldn't bring himself to feel annoyed.

At the moment, nothing else mattered but keeping her safe.

TWENTY-THREE

It took them hours to find the cabin. By then, it was past midnight, and Serana was grateful they hadn't been mauled by lions, tigers, or whatever the hell lurked in these woods.

Almost as grateful as she was for the fact that Logan stayed by her side the entire time.

To be fair, the reasonable thing would be to drive her to the nearest hospital—and his terse frown warned he wanted to. All he did was follow the mountain road deeper into the forest surrounding Meyweather. He didn't even argue when her confusion with the directions led them to several dead ends.

Now that they were here, she didn't know what to do. Fingers shaking, she tried to grab her bag from the back seat, only to have Logan snatch it from her grip.

"Come on."

She followed him up a short dirt path leading to a square cabin. It was larger than she had imagined—the size of a decent house, rather than the shack she'd pictured.

As she crept up beside Logan, she eased her bag from his grip to fish out her keys. It took her a few tries to find the right one amid the many belonging to her father, but a large silver one did the trick.

"Wait here," Logan told her, before delving head-first into the darkness alone.

A part of her railed at the whole *me Tarzan, you Jane* aspect of him being the big brave man by checking out the cabin first—but it was dark, and the weaving branches seemed a little more sinister bathed in the gray light of the moon.

Eventually, his voice came from the shadows. "Serana." A split second later, yellow light pierced the darkness as he presumably flicked a switch. "It's alright. You can come in."

With a sigh of relief, Serana slipped inside and closed the door behind her. The main room sported an open floor plan. At the far end, Logan stood beside a massive stone fireplace surrounded by a few pieces of simple, yet sturdy furniture.

The other half of the space held a decent kitchen, and a narrow hallway branched off to two closed doors.

"Looks like there's only one bedroom," he said while setting her duffle on the floor beside a solid-oak coffee table. "I'll sleep on the couch."

Serana froze, unsure if she'd heard him right. "You mean… you're s-staying here?"

"Yes." He cocked an eyebrow, his eyes an unsettling hue of emerald. "Of course, I am. Unless you were actually planning on staying here by yourself, in which case I'd have to wonder—are you insane?"

Point taken. Now that she was here, Serana certainly didn't feel capable of staying this far out in the woods, alone.

Still…

"Logan, I'm fine," she lied, avoiding his gaze. "I can take care of myself—"

"Oh, really?" He was in front of her in an instant, palming her chin. "You. Look. Like. Shit. Come here."

Before Serana could resist the contact, he lifted her off her feet, carried her to the couch, and set her down.

"Don't move," he warned before heading to the kitchen, where Serana could hear him rummaging through cabinets and opening the fridge. A moment later, he reappeared, holding an awkward bundle that he pressed beneath her chin.

"Keep it there," he ordered, before turning away again.

Serana raised her head as far as she dared to watch him. Whatever she held beneath her jaw was refreshingly cool—a makeshift ice pack, she saw, glancing down. Probably just a bag of ice from the freezer bundled in what looked like…

Oh. Her mind barely registered the dark covering of her ice pack as the same dark-blue color of his shirt—until she saw that he suddenly wasn't wearing one.

Oh my...

Her throat went dry at the sight of him, chest bared, muscles rippling beneath his skin. Despite the mess that had become of today, for just a brief moment, she could forget it all as he searched the cupboards like a man on a mission.

"What are you looking for?" she asked around her throbbing jaw.

"Food," he said. "Let's hope you don't have a concussion, but you need something in your stomach at least."

Serana shook her head. "I'm not hungry."

She expected him to argue. Maybe try to shove an old box of crackers she could see at the back of one of the cupboards down her throat. Instead, all he did was return to her side.

"How do you feel?"

She hesitated before answering. Her jaw ached from where she'd hit it off the steering wheel, and she could only hope, like he did, that she didn't have a concussion.

In the end, she couldn't bring herself to answer, and just watched him instead, awed by how the lamp light played off the gold in his skin. He observed her in return, only he didn't seem to be in awe of her beauty. Just worried.

"You look…" He brushed a warm finger against her forehead. Though he never put an adjective to what exactly she looked like, judging from the concern shaping his mouth, she could guess.

"I'm fine—"

"No." Logan cut her off with a firm bit of pressure on her bottom lip. "You're not. Don't move."

Once again, he returned to the kitchen and came back with a wad of paper towels in one hand. "Don't move," he repeated, before applying gentle pressure to the worst of the bruising.

Serana endured his ministrations in silence, trying to ignore just how distracting it was to have him so close. Distracting from the pain. Distracting from…

Everything.

Did the guy take lessons from Florence Nightingale or something? His touch was downright therapeutic, betraying a familiarity with violence.

"You can tell me the truth," she croaked. "Were you really in prison?"

That would certainly explain his skill with makeshift first-aid supplies. Considering that he carried a talking knife, she could only imagine the danger he was used to encountering.

"I'm not the one with head trauma." He sighed, avoiding her gaze. "Why the hell didn't I take you to the hospital?"

Serana shrugged. "Maybe I'm not the only one who's going insane?"

"Maybe," she thought she heard him grunt. But she could have been hallucinating...

She felt delirious enough to be. Stars danced across her vision as Logan gently wiped one last smear of blood from her forehead.

"You get some rest," he said, tossing the tissue onto the coffee table. "I'll keep an eye out."

Serana tried to stand, but it was harder to put into practice. She was forced to grab onto the nearest solid thing, which happened to be Logan's arm.

He waited until she tried to take a step and threw his other arm around her waist, pressing her to his chest. Serana couldn't silence a groan. He was so warm. Nothing like the frigid chill that seemed to permeate everything else she touched. When she braced her palm against his chest, she felt some semblance of clarity pierce her thoughts for the first time since Zoe's unwelcome appearance.

"I shouldn't go to sleep," she murmured, surprised by how steady her voice sounded. "If I have a concussion."

"Then, you shouldn't sleep," he agreed, before setting her down on the couch.

Serana didn't know what was wrong with her. Only earlier that day, she had attacked the guy with a blade, and now... She couldn't fight the urge that had her reaching out for him, grabbing his arm.

"Just…stay with me. Please. I don't want to be alone."

Logan didn't answer. He stood there for so long she wondered if the man was getting a cramp, before a sudden impulse had her shifting over, revealing a sliver of space beside her.

"Come lay with me."

A heartbeat later, he relented, sliding an arm beneath her waist to hold her close. "I'm going to burn in Hell for this."

Burn.

Serana liked the idea a lot. A whole lot—especially as two warm fingers caressed her arm, leaving a delicious trail of heat.

"You aren't used to this," she suspected, reading the truth concealed in his tense posture. "Lying with someone without sex involved."

Did that reveal just how much of a shallow playboy he truly was? No. She sensed it alluded to a far more personal truth regarding Logan—there were few people in his life he'd ever trusted enough to relax in their presence, even for a second.

If her suspicion held any truth to it, his reaction gave her no sign. He grunted a noise that could be interpreted as a laugh. "No. I think I've told you before, but most people—"

"Either want to fuck you or kill you," she finished softly. Could it be that what she first interpreted as cocky bravado was more or less a sad reflection of how he viewed himself?

Someone capable only of being lusted after or destroyed, there was no in-between. "You've never had a relationship before?"

He took a while before answering with a sigh. "No. I've never been interested in one, to be honest."

But that wasn't the full truth. Taking a stab in the dark, she asked, "Too busy bouncing in and out of prison?"

"You could say that," he admitted. "Trouble has a way of finding me, whether I like it or not."

Her heart panged at the hint of sadness in his voice. She suspected that it bothered him to reveal even a sliver of weakness to her. He had anyway.

"Tell me about it."

He went silent again. If he iced her out completely, would that bother her? Maybe.

Just as doubt crept in, he finally opened his mouth.

"I don't know much about my family. My mother... Wasn't around much when I was growing up. A few months ago, I learned of something that might provide more insight, so I tried to, ah—'borrow' it."

"You mean you stole it," she surmised.

"Something like that. I *tried* to steal it from someone very powerful, and a man died in the aftermath. I didn't want it to happen. It just... Did."

A fantastical story. The scary part? She believed him—all of it. If anything, he seemed to be deliberately curtailing the details. Out of shame? No one could fake the raw note in his voice. This was a side of him she sensed he never revealed to anyone. The fact that she was allowed to glimpse it was merely due to an oversight on his part—he had let his guard down around her.

And she didn't dare take that for granted, not even for a second.

"Why come to Meyweather?" she asked, rather than press him for more details. This moment felt way too fragile to give him the third degree.

He shrugged, his gaze pensive. "Marcus offered me a fresh start, so I took him up on it. That's all there is."

"A rather short story," she teased.

"Well, you told me that I should keep you awake," Logan grumbled by way of explanation. "Apart from my bullshit backstory, how exactly am I supposed to do that?"

There wasn't anything overly sexual in the man's tone—for once. But Serana couldn't ignore the electric charge that seemed to spark in the air between them, making her skin sizzle.

What appealed to her more than learning snippets of his past? Perhaps, exploring his body in a way she had yet to, even during their so-called one-night stand.

"Don't play coy now." She released a shaky laugh, surprising herself. "I'm sure you can think of plenty of ways."

She felt Logan stiffen. Of course, he would have picked up on the unspoken innuendo. But...was that what she really meant? It only took Serana a second to decide.

Oh yes. Maybe not full-on sex...

That would imply she most definitely had a concussion. *But touching?* She shivered at the thought of feeling his searing heat all over her body. Touching was *definitely* an option—platonically speaking, of course.

Eager to test her theory, she shifted to face him directly.

Heavy lidded with confusion, his eyes burned, matching the intensity Serana felt run through her. Gently, he stroked a stray curl from her face, and raw, delicious heat lanced through her as the pad of his thumb slid against her skin.

Pull back Serana, a part of her scolded. *You're delirious.*

Ignoring the warning, she palmed his bare chest with both hands while wiggling closer, eager to leech off his warmth. Logan stiffened at her touch, but Serana had a feeling his discomfort had more to do with the firm bulge forming against her belly.

Was the guy *always* turned on?

No, something told her as those green eyes deepened into a dusky emerald. *Not always...*

Danger, a part of Serana warned from the back of her mind as Logan shifted closer. *Earth to Serana. Reel it in before...*

Before what?

He couldn't exactly kiss her, with her jaw aching like she'd lost a fight with a tire iron. At least, he couldn't kiss her on the mouth.

"Logan," she whispered, voice so husky and raw it almost hurt to talk. "No strings attached, remember? So, this doesn't count."

For once, she didn't worry about guilt, shame, or embarrassment as she reached between them to cup him where it counted.

A muscle jerked in Logan's jaw, and he held her gaze for so long she wondered if he'd decided that she indeed had a concussion and was contemplating dragging her back into his truck and straight to the hospital. Though, that little theory was all but demolished when he leaned against her, placing his mouth near her ear to whisper huskily, "This doesn't count, either."

He moved—making sure her hand never left contact—to roll on top of her while supporting the brunt of his weight with an elbow propped beside her head. His mouth found the crook of her shoulder, and the heat of his breath goaded her to brush her hand against him in a single stroke. His guttural reply made Serana shiver, biting her lip as he swelled against her touch.

"Mmmm." It was the only sound she could make as her fingers brushed him slow and steady—she had no warning, but a hoarse growl before Logan returned the favor, reaching down to stroke her heatedly through her jeans. The conflicting sensation of the harshness of denim on flesh made her breath hitch in her throat.

Her legs sprung apart, freeing him to explore her further, while her own hand squeezed him through the confines of his jeans.

She could feel that heat rising up hard and fast, just like it had in the bar. Was she willing to follow this to wherever it might lead?

One look at him was all it took.

Oh yes.

Serana barely felt in control of her own limbs as she released her grip on him to drag both hands desperately down her front. Arching her hips against him, she flicked the clasp of her jeans.

"Logan…"

He hissed a strangled sound against her neck that could have been her name, and snatched her wrist as she started to fumble with the zipper. "Can't," she heard him grunt, a little more legibly this time. "Concussion."

Somewhere at the back of her mind, Serana knew he was right. That didn't make it feel any less satisfying to grasp the fingers of his hand and pull it down right where she wanted him to be.

A moan tore from her throat at the sharp, burning heat that rose beneath his touch. Her hips jerked against him, her trembling grip still holding him captive.

His name was the only sound she could make beneath a rush of desire that swamped her with the need to feel him against her—any way she could.

With a growl he pulled his hands away, but before her throat could even form a disappointed moan, those fingers were back, tugging at her pants and wrenching aside her panties to plunge deep.

Serana's mind went blank. She stopped thinking or feeling anything but pure, satisfying pleasure as he took her with a sharp jab from his thumb. She rocked her hips, desperate to take him deeper, harder—but the touch was only a tease, never deepening more than that.

The bastard was trying to be a gentleman. Another time, she might have appreciated the caution. Not *now*.

Ignoring the pain in her jaw, she gritted her teeth and cupped the man completely in the center of her palm. Shock made him jump, distracting him long enough for her other hand to undo the clasp of his jeans.

Holy…goodness gracious. Even felt through touch, she knew he was well-endowed. Only now could she appreciate just *how* well, with the heat of him springing hard and hot against her stomach. A delicious sense of curiosity had her aching to free him from the fabric of his boxers to see all of him.

"No strings," she whispered, almost on a plea, before sliding her hand beneath his waistband. "*Please*, Logan."

He made a sound she had never heard a human make before at her touch. Or maybe it was just that she was practically begging him for…

Hell, she didn't even know just what she was begging for. All she knew was the incredible sensation of velvet encasing molten steel as she brushed him with the tips of her fingers.

Thunder. That's all she heard—all she felt. Just a rippling sensation that rumbled all the way down her spine as the world shifted. The next moment she found herself straddling Logan as he tore her jeans down her legs and threw them aside.

"No strings," he repeated, almost in a chant, wrenching her against his chest by her waist, but not before returning her hand to the bulge straining through the fly in his jeans.

Serana sighed at the feel of him. Had he grown even harder in the short space of time? She stroked him eagerly, aching to shrug off his boxers and find out.

"Good God, Serana."

She glanced up to find him staring at her with smoldering eyes. There was pure reverence in that gaze as it swept over the hair falling down her shoulders to the bared skin of her belly and thighs.

"You are so fucking beautiful."

For the first time in her life, Serana believed it. Even with her face bruised and swollen and her eyes still sore from tears.

She believed *him*.

Maybe it was just shock from the accident still addling her brain?

Or his heat was just driving her mad?

Or just the simple fact that she didn't give a damn as she brought a trembling hand around the back of his neck and eased herself closer?

She wished more than anything that she could kiss him— feel those soft lips on her own. Instead, she nuzzled the good side of her face against the crook of his neck. His smell wafted against her nose—honey, cloves, and the sweet scent of spice.

Good God, she needed him *now*. Her jaw felt too tender to speak, so she let her hand say exactly what she wanted without words. Logan made a coarse sound of agreement at the back of his throat.

"No sex," he grunted, shocking her. Before Serana could protest, he flipped her back onto the cushion and hovered above her waist. "No sex," he promised, before leaning down to swipe the panties from her legs.

Serana wondered what the hell "no sex" could mean with her pants off—until she felt the warmth of his thumb brush her, just once.

Right before he lowered his head…

She didn't know what to expect—foreplay hadn't exactly been on the table during her short teenage romance, and the few moments with Logan, while scorching, had *nothing* on this.

She slapped a hand over her mouth, wincing at the sharp pain that followed. But it was minimal compared to the heart-stopping anticipation that rushed to replace it. Warm breath engulfed her, as he hesitated for only a second, before gently latching his lips over the center of her core.

It was like fire. She jerked, fingers turning into claws that tore through his hair as the moist heat of his mouth ravaged her.

He kissed her *there* with almost the same vigor that he did her mouth. Licking, tasting…sucking. It was all Serana could do to just lie back and try to keep from being knocked under.

Try to keep her sanity as she forgot about Zoe, her father, and everything else.

It was like the numbing bliss of alcohol—times a thousand.

"Logan." His name was a prayer on her lips—the only word she could form. "*Logan!*"

Her hips bucked against him, urging him deeper, harder, offering all she was. In response, his hand slid beneath her sweater, ghosting the top of her stomach before inching higher.

There was a soft snap as her bra came undone, allowing those wicked fingers to cup the mound of her breast. Serana groaned at the sensation, whimpering as the pad of his thumb struck the peak of a nipple, sending a shock lancing through her.

At the same moment, his mouth broke free. Hot breath teasing her stomach through her sweater was all she felt as he pressed a kiss over the fabric. At the same time, he replaced his tongue with the firm ridge of a finger, sinking deep.

Serana couldn't take it. She was shaking, rocking her hips back and forth in tune with the rhythm he urged with every thrust of his hand. Her moans seemed to goad him, those green eyes latching onto hers as he toyed with the flat of her belly.

"That's it," he urged, his voice a deep, rasping tenor. "Let go."

The words were like striking a match on a bit of tinder. Serana lurched as a massive inferno of pleasure swept over her body like a brushfire. She couldn't breathe. Couldn't think.

Her only shred of sense was to throw a hand behind her, bracing herself against the armrest of the couch as she...

Came apart.

Nothing. Nothing in the whole world could possibly compare to this—compare to him. Serana almost ached at the thought of the rules to their little arrangement—*no strings.*

She wanted more. Would *always* want more. It was getting hard to even remember why she *shouldn't*, as she rode that glorious wave of ecstasy.

Logan stroked her through it all, sliding in and out of the liquid lust that built between her thighs to ease his entrance. For what seemed like a million torturous years, he never stopped, only sped up—until, with one last moan, Serana quaked and went silent.

For a long moment, she could only lay there, panting as Logan finally eased his hand from her.

"Are you alright?"

She nodded, loving the hoarse concern in his voice. Loving the heat that pricked at her belly and the exhaustion of pure bliss that blotted out all thought of anything else. Would she regret this tomorrow?

Probably.

She couldn't bring herself to care as she reached up to loop an arm around Logan's neck. He allowed the contact, but surprised her by turning her onto her side and lying beside her.

"I promised not to let you fall asleep," he said against her ear. The firmness of his thighs pressed against hers as he wrapped an arm tight around her waist. "I'm afraid I've ensured the opposite."

Serana laughed, utterly at ease as she relaxed into his grip. "Don't worry," she whispered, even as her eyes slid shut. "If I don't wake up…I'm sure you'll find a way…"

She was almost tempted to test that little theory. For the first time, the thought of tomorrow was a delicious treat that lingered at the back of her mind as she finally surrendered to exhaustion.

TWENTY-FOUR

Logan gazed at Serana's slumbering body and hated himself. Instead of getting the hell away from her, like he *should* have, all he could picture were the sweet sounds she'd made as she shuddered in the throes of her climax.

One he'd raised to life with his tongue.

Shit. She could have fallen into a coma for all he knew, but for some reason, he couldn't bring himself to wake her. She looked so damn peaceful, and he stood before he was tempted to do something stupid. Like test her little theory from last night about how to wake her up if he was worried…

Instead, he grabbed Serana's duffle. Inside, amid a mound of clothes, he found a box of matches which he slipped into his pocket.

The fireplace seemed functional, and after a quick peek out of the front door, he caught sight of a stack of wood and an ax. Not far from the cabin was a stump that he used to slice the logs in half.

The busy work gave him a distraction. Something to take his mind off the woman lying peacefully only a few yards away.

It didn't take much of the pale morning light to tell that Serana's face was a bruised, swollen mess. She looked like hell, and while he'd found a blanket in the night to cover them both with, the sight of her bare toes peeking from beneath the thick cotton made something like guilt pinch in his gut.

There was no way around it—he had taken advantage of her. Crushed against her on the couch, he'd let lust override common sense. His only comfort was that he hadn't fully taken her how he'd longed to—especially with the fresh box of condoms in his truck.

Still. He'd kept his promise. Though, it was getting harder to remember exactly why that was a *good* thing as the front of his jeans tightened.

He had enough wood for a fire in no time, and it was almost reluctantly that he headed back into the cabin with the wood in tow.

"Morning." The quiet greeting drew his attention to the stove where Serana stood stirring something in a metal pot she must have fished from one of the cabinets. An empty can of soup sat nearby.

"Morning," Logan replied, noticing that she'd changed into a pair of sweatpants. Her hair was unbound, but the dark strands weren't enough to distract from the fact that her face was a beautiful mess of ivory, purple, and ebony.

Ass, Logan scolded himself. She looked horrible and sore, and he just hoped the deep cut on her forehead didn't need stitches.

Awkwardly, he hefted the firewood to the fireplace. With the aid of some old newspapers, he quickly had a good blaze. The task didn't take nearly the time he wished it had.

It was too soon that he had to turn and face Serana, who'd curled up on the couch, sipping her soup from an old coffee mug. Those gray eyes stared impassively, just…watching.

"I thought you'd left," she said after a moment, surprising him. "I wouldn't blame you if you had."

"I'm not that much of an asshole." He shrugged, reached for an iron poker hanging on a hook above the mantel, and began stoking the embers. "If that's what you were hoping for, you can just stop—because I'm not leaving you here."

"Why?"

The soft question threw him off.

The truth—*I was drawn to you subconsciously because my knife chose you as its beholder*—probably wouldn't fly.

"What happened to push you off that road?" he asked, changing the subject.

There was a sharp intake of breath. "I swerved to avoid a bird—"

"No." He turned around, forcing himself to meet those gray eyes head-on. "Before that."

She flinched, fingers shaking as they cupped her mug of soup. She was silent for so long he thought she wouldn't answer. Then…

"I was upset," she began softly. "Someone I haven't seen in a while came back unannounced with some not-so-good news."

"A lover?" He tried to keep *what* out of his voice—annoyance? Irritation? God forbid, jealousy?

"No," she murmured. "A stepsister."

With one last jab at the fire, he set the poker aside and faced her, bracing his hands on his knees. As he waited, she placed her mug on the coffee table and tucked a strand of hair behind her ear.

"My mother died when I was eight," she began with a sigh. "It didn't take long for my father to get married again—he'd been cheating on her for years anyway. But the woman he chose was kind, and she had a daughter near my age, named Zoe." Serana shifted on the couch, drawing her knees up to her chin.

"Despite all the rumors about stepsisters, Zoe was my best friend. She was older and smart and pretty, and I looked up to her. Growing up in my father's house, I had always been alone, but during that short time, I wasn't…"

She trailed off, staring into space as if tormented by the memories. Logan found himself moving closer, sitting on the edge of the couch.

"What happened?" He forced himself to ask.

She lifted her shoulders in a shrug. "Like he did with everyone else, my father grew distant from his new wife. They divorced three years later and moved across the country when his ex-wife found work. Zoe promised to visit, but she never did until last night...when she showed up on my doorstep to let me know that the one thing of value I'd thought my father had left me, wasn't really mine after all."

She released a hard laugh that held so much pain it made Logan's throat ache.

"Tell me," he coaxed.

"He'd left part of the house to her, and who knows what else—that's why I couldn't stay there..."

Logan didn't know what to say. He felt a strange inclination to do something instead. Hold her? Hug her? Either reaction wouldn't be a very good idea—despite whatever had happened between them last night, she didn't seem to take physical contact very well.

So, he just stayed by her side, watching the fire lick at the wood.

"I didn't mean to call you," she admitted after a moment. "It's just...I couldn't think of anyone else...and your number was in my phone, and I just..."

She trailed off, and Logan was almost grateful for the resulting silence.

"It's alright," he said truthfully. "I would have spent the night helping Marcus with the bar anyway."

Speaking of the brooding Raeth, it would probably be a good idea to inform him of his and Serana's current whereabouts.

"I should go to his place and get some food, at least. If you're still here when I get back…" He trailed off, not really sure what he meant. "I'll *be* back. Now that I know how to find this place, I should be gone an hour tops. I'll bring you some clothes, too."

"Okay." Serana nodded as he reluctantly headed for the door.

"Wait!" He turned to find her pointing to an object lying on the floor beside the couch—a leather sheath with Krall tucked inside. How the hell he hadn't noticed it last night—Logan had no idea.

But he certainly recognized the hilt of Krall alright, poking from the black material. His fingers itched for his blade, but somehow, he managed to find the strength to keep from reaching for it.

"I still have your knife." She looked guilty at that fact as she began to pull Krall free. "D-do you want it?"

That blond witch, Hazel's words ran through Logan's mind before he could help it—*She is the beholder of your weapon whether you like it or not. Though, if you truly wanted to get rid of her, I suppose you could just let her die…*

"Why don't you hold onto it?" he found himself stammering. "Just for a while?"

Serana slid Krall back into that sheath a little more eagerly than he figured most women would the weapon of a complete stranger.

He wanted to ask her—but something told him that now, when she was in the midst of her own drama, was not the time.

Even *he* had tact.

Though, being around her seemed to obliterate it. He spared her battered form one last glance, before wrenching open the door and slipping out as if Hell were on his heels.

TWENTY-FIVE

Serana didn't know what to do once Logan left. She needed to shower, comb her hair, and call Mirabelle before the woman went ballistic—but other than that, she didn't know what to *do*.

Should she stay? Not that she exactly had many places to go, deep in the forest without a car. But still…

The thought of Logan coming back made her…giddy. Petrified. Terrified. Excited. Every possible emotion a woman could feel bubbled inside her, all at once. The most horrific realization of all?

She *wanted* him to come back.

Was that so wrong? *Yes,* a part of her hissed. *You've done fine this far alone.* But that was the thing. She was tired of being alone. Tired of having no one. Tired of…

Being like her father.

It had been nice to have company, if only to participate in some hasty foreplay on the couch of a strange cabin in the middle of the woods. The fact of the matter was that Logan, for whatever reason, had been there. Taken care of her. Comforted her in the only way he seemed to know how.

Sure, the guy was an unapologetic horn-dog—but it worked. For now, at least, she wasn't worried about Zoe or anyone else.

Instead, all she cared about was when she'd see him again.

You've got to get him out of your blood, girl, a part of her warned. *You can't afford to let someone like him in.*

Logan didn't exactly seem like the commitment type, but Serana couldn't resist wondering if that was part of the allure. Wanting a relationship with him was like wishing on a star or admiring a celebrity from afar.

As strong as the desire may be, there was always a part of her that knew, deep down, that nothing would ever come out of it.

It was safe. Or…

She shivered at the thought of his fingers warm and soft on her skin, and that incredible heat.

Maybe, *not* so safe.

Trembling, Serana stood and dragged her duffle past the kitchen and tried one of the closed doors until she found a decent-sized bathroom with an unexpected Jacuzzi tub.

Obviously, this little cabin wasn't so rustic after all.

She tried not to imagine the type of women her father might have brought out here—if any—as she stripped her beer-covered sweater and climbed into the tub. The hot water was a blessing, and she turned the faucet on high and sat back, allowing the heat to wash over her aching, sore limbs.

She didn't know how long she stayed there, breathing in the steam. It had to be sometime later when she finally climbed out and wrapped herself in a towel.

Somehow, in her haphazard packing, she'd taken the essential toiletries—her toothbrush, a tube of toothpaste, and a pair of sweats. Once dressed, she found herself strapping Krall's sheath to her waist, though she chose not to examine the reasoning behind it.

After scraping her hair into a bun, she found her cell phone and dialed the clinic. Mirabelle picked up on the first ring. "Hello?"

"It's me," Serana began, but Mirabelle cut her off before she could get another word out.

"Serana?" There was a sharp intake of breath and then a harsh sigh. "Serana, what the hell is wrong with you? Do you have any idea how *worried* I've been?" Mirabelle's tone was an uncharacteristic hiss. "When you didn't show up for work, I tried calling you, thinking that maybe you were still sick. Then I went to your house…"

Oh. Serana winced, slapping her free hand across the uninjured part of her forehead. "I sort of…left town for a while."

"I could tell when I saw your car wasn't in the garage," Mirabelle replied sarcastically. "Is it so hard for you to let someone in? Let people know before you just skip town in the middle of the night like some—"

Abruptly the woman broke off, keeping herself from finishing that sentence. "Tell me where you are so I can see for myself that you haven't been kidnapped and aren't just speaking to me under duress."

Serana winced. "I can't."

Not with her face looking like she'd been partially put through a meat grinder.

"But I'm safe," she said quickly. "And I'm sorry—I just needed…a break."

There was a heavy sigh from the other end. "Can you at least tell me where you are?"

Serana thought for a moment. "One of my father's old cabins."

"Where?"

"Near the mountains," she said evasively. As much as she appreciated Mirabelle's concern, she doubted the woman wouldn't rush her to a hospital when she saw her face. "Please," she added, surprised by how her voice shook. "I just really need to be away from people right now. Please… don't be angry with me."

She was surprised by how much the thought bothered her. Out of everyone, Mirabelle was one of the few who seemed genuinely concerned about her for whatever reason.

"I'm not mad," the woman insisted. "I'm just… The next time you decide to skip town without notice, can you please let someone know first?"

"Of course," Serana said, unwilling to mention that someone *did* know about her little trip.

"And next time, please don't wait until you feel the need to just disappear to take a break—anyone with eyes could have seen how stressed you were with everything going on."

Had she been stressed? Serana frowned as she tried to picture her emotions these past few days—whatever they were, they hadn't exactly been pleasant.

"Sure thing," she promised to Mirabelle. "You'll be the first to know. By the way, thank you for the soup—I feel better already."

"No problem," Mirabelle replied, sounding a bit calmer. "Though, if you tell me where you are, I could always bring you more."

"Nice try." Serana laughed, even though there wasn't any real joy in it. "I'll be back in town soon—I promise. Until then, do you mind covering the clinic for me?"

"Of course! You just…take care, wherever you are, okay?"

"Sure thing—"

The sound of knocking on the door made Serana break off. "I have to go," she said to Mirabelle, pulling the cell phone away from her ear.

She wondered if Logan had come back already—why that thought made an excited bit of energy prickle her stomach?

She had no idea.

Her fingers shook as she palmed the doorknob and twisted.

"Logan? I told you, you didn't have to…"

She trailed off as fear encircled her throat. The man standing on the other end, while gloriously tall and blond, was *not* Logan.

Dark blue eyes took her in with a feral sweep, settling on the sheath strapped to her waist where Krall rested.

"Well." He had a voice like the ocean—as heavy as a tempest crashing upon the shore. "You are certainly *not* my brother."

TWENTY-SIX

Logan drove straight to the pub, but getting food for the cabin wasn't his sole concern. Serana claimed a bird had caused her to veer off the road, but what if his mysterious jailbreakers were behind it?

In which case, he should have never left her alone in the woods, miles from civilization to begin with.

Right. Eager to rectify that fact, he parked in the alley and entered through the kitchen.

To his surprise, Marcus was already awake, washing dishes in the industrial-style kitchen. From the stern set to his shoulders, Logan sensed that a desire to start work wasn't the reason for his early rising.

Uh-oh.

"You lied to me," he said before Logan could even question his demeanor. "About why you were really in prison."

Logan flinched. So maybe he'd skimmed on the details regarding his prison break. Marcus didn't seem like the nosy type. "Look, maybe I embellished a bit—"

"Perhaps lie is too strong a word," Marcus clarified without turning around. His tone revealed he wasn't angry. Merely curious. "You deliberately left out a crucial detail regarding the charges on your head. Who you stole from, for example, and what you were after."

Oh. That. Logan shifted uneasily from foot to foot. Did he particularly care to admit the truth behind his grand theft scheme or that the cause was a few bad dreams? Not really. When someone attempted to steal from a daemon lord, one might think their quarry would be something worth the risk. Untold riches. Vast, magical artifacts. Or, in his case…

"You want the full story? Fine. I heard he had something that can predict the future. I wanted to know mine," he confessed. All in all, a rather pathetic mission. Certainly not brazen enough to put Marcus on edge.

With a sigh, Marcus set his wet rag aside and turned from the sink. "This changes things," he said. "I assumed your motives would be selfish, but if you were willing to bet your life on such a farfetched hope, you must have had good intel."

Logan took offense to the characterization. "Not perfect, but it was better than stalking the harbinger waiting for the doom to begin. Rumor has it Donovan's been hosting powerful daemons. I'm talking, council-level powerful, and he's bribing them with access to some sort of future-telling device. Something like that might come in handy if the apocalypse truly is upon us."

And help Logan understand if he might be the cause of it all.

Marcus raised an eyebrow. "You stole from Donovan?"

The daemon lord had quite the reputation for being a psychopath and a ruthless enforcer of his realm—two things that were a damn near requirement when it came to owning such a title. What made Donny special was his skill as a Klaen. If a daemon gang leader wanted to one-up a rival, he went to the unofficial kingmaker and groveled. No one had more influence throughout most of Hell.

So yeah, perhaps Marcus' skepticism was warranted.

"*Tried* to steal," Logan clarified. "I got into the fortress, but I didn't find shit. Not a secret room of treasure. No magic crystal ball. If the man has such a device, he keeps it close."

"Or," Marcus said softly, stroking his chin. "It isn't a device at all."

"You believe me?" Logan threw his hands up in exasperation. "Then why the third degree?"

"Because if it's true, the consequences are far-reaching," his brother explained, his expression serious. "Liva seems to have an uncanny knack of always being one step ahead. I've wondered why that is."

Logan cocked his head, suspicious. "It sounds like you've seen her recently."

"Not me personally," Marcus admitted. "But someone I know. Liva may just be a meticulous planner, but I think the more likely explanation is that she's coordinating with something or someone. Learning what parts of her plan are ready to come to fruition and where."

"I don't like the sound of that," Logan said.

"Exactly, which is why I reached out to Jacelyn," Marcus explained, referring to their reclusive brother. "He's on his way here, but he mentioned that your name is on the lips of every bounty hunter in Hell. Donovan, it seems, hasn't agreed with your sudden release from prison. He wants you dead."

"Great," Logan hissed. "A daemon lord wants me dead, and my fucking knife left me for a woman. What next?"

"What next is you elaborate on your intel regarding Donovan's device, and we aim to retrieve it. I've heard similar rumors, but I think now may be the time to act."

"You know what it is, don't you?" Logan asked, seeing through his vague language.

"No," Marcus said carefully. "I think I know who. Donovan is a powerful Klaen, from a strong bloodline. Who better than to co-opt said bloodline for her own means than our dear old mother?"

"You think Donovan has one of us?"

It was a horrifying concept Logan didn't even want to consider.

"I think we need to find out before someone else attempts to steal whatever or whoever this device may be. And," Marcus added, "we need to figure out how best to handle Serana. She is a good woman. I don't want to see her hurt."

Logan recoiled at the genuine concern in his voice. "Why is that? Because you want her for yourself?"

Wow. Was that jealousy? He didn't get jealous. He never got attached to anyone long enough to be. But with Serana…

The thought of her writhing beneath Marcus made a sour taste lurch onto his tongue, and he curled a fist before he could help it.

"No," his brother said softly, dispelling some of his anger. "But I respect her, and she's been through too much hell this year to have you come along and fuck with her emotions."

Logan flinched. "I'm not fucking with her emotions." Not that he didn't exactly want to utilize that verb with other parts of her body.

"Whatever is going on between us is none of your damn business," he grumbled before his brother could reply. "Still, I'm flattered that you think I'm so much of an asshole you need to be concerned for the women I sleep with."

"Not all of them," Marcus replied, equally as soft. "And trust me, Logan—I am not half as worried for Serana as I am for you—you're falling for her."

"I am *not* falling for her," Logan all but scoffed, even as an impulse to return to her flared up so strongly he had to stop himself from leaving now.

Something he would have never considered with any other woman. Hell, even though a majority of it was just foreplay, he'd never shared half as much of his body or time with another woman.

Deep inside, his own instincts were screaming at him to be careful. *Pull back.* That spending any more time with Serana would be treading on dangerous ground.

But a larger part of him didn't really give a shit.

"I've only known her for like, four days," he muttered as an excuse.

"Oh, really?" Marcus said, crossing his arms. "Well, either way, you'll need to form some kind of relationship with her as you figure out what to do about Krall. Are you going to tell her the truth? About us—about *everything*? You remember what Hazel said—"

"Yeah, I remember," Logan snapped. "But I still don't see why I should have to listen to that preteen. What's her deal anyway?"

He wasn't referring to the witch's powers. He still remembered what Marcus had said as they'd left the girl's cabin, "she's our sister…"

He hadn't been in the mood to ask many questions at the time. The idea that Liva, their so-called "mother," had more children left a bad taste in his mouth. How many half-breeds were out there running around sired by only God knew who?

Or what, he added, thinking of Jace and Mirabelle with a grimace.

"I think Hazel may be the last," Marcus said, as if reading his mind. "She's only sixteen."

"Let's hope she's the last of us," Logan said, but he wasn't optimistic.

"Despite her age, Hazel has been trained by some of the best witches of this age," Marcus went on. "She knows a thing or two about daemons, so when it comes to Serana and Krall, I suggest you listen."

Logan frowned and marched over to the bar to fish a bottle of something strong from the shelf above the sink. He sensed Marcus on his heels, silently watching.

"What the hell am I supposed to do? Tell her the truth about everything—'Hey Serana, you know those things that go *bump* in the night—they're called daemons, and I'm one of them. By the way, my ancient, enchanted blade has *bound* itself to you, for whatever reason. Wanna go get a drink, and I'll tell ya all about it?'"

He shot Marcus an exasperated glance from over his shoulder.

"Maybe not so sarcastically," his brother murmured. "But something close enough. She deserves to know the truth, Logan. Perhaps if you weren't so busy trying to sleep with her, you could see that."

Logan scoffed, though he couldn't ignore the guilt pinching his gut. Thanks to his carelessness with Krall, Serana was dragged into his mess.

Still.

"I don't think one little knife is cause to give the woman a lifetime of nightmares." After all, a few months of disturbed sleep had driven him to attempt to steal from a daemon lord and get thrown in prison. "If Mirabelle doesn't need to know, then neither does Serana."

"Fine," Marcus said with a nod. "But, you still need to decide what you're going to do about—"

"Hold on." Logan snatched for his cell phone as his pocket buzzed with the vibration of an incoming call. He answered without glancing at the caller ID—anything to distract from Marcus' conversation—and nearly dropped the damn phone altogether.

"Where is he?" The voice on the other end sounded muffled, as if heard from underwater. Logan didn't recognize the deep tones, but he recognized the pathetic whimper that came in answer alright.

Serana.

She was in danger.

TWENTY-SEVEN

oincidence was a luxury a daemon hunter of Jace's caliber couldn't afford. After searching for his brothers, who should he find but a lone woman in the middle of the woods, sporting Logan's blade. That alone didn't bode well. The mystery only deepened at the sound of his brother's name on her lips.

Damn. What had that idiot of a Shael done now?

Something far worse than petty theft if the rumors circulating the underworld were to be believed. As far as his newfound family went, at least Jace knew he wasn't the fuck-up of the bunch.

"Who are you?" the woman demanded. Her fingers tightened over the door handle, and Jace knew she was about seconds from closing it. "What do you want?"

What did he want?

Answers. Answers to why Logan Merris' name seemed to be on every daemon hunter's lips with an enormous bounty attached. Perhaps there were more selfish reasons mingled amongst that desire. Like a need to meet her—*his* sister. His twin.

To be fair, when he'd blown his brothers off the first time, disbelief had less to do with it and more of the fact that daemon hunting left little time for family reunions. Did he believe his mother had been a fucking slut who'd sired children with as many daemons as she could find?

Sure.

Did he believe his twin sister held a power capable of saving or destroying the world?

Maybe.

Either way, he had more important shit to do than wait around to find out. Until now. The daemon world was rumbling with unease. When the last daemon he'd hunted down beneath a city overpass had gleefully told him that the world was coming to an end, right before his throat was slit, Jace decided it was time to stop fucking around and get some answers.

He'd already been in the mortal realm when Marcus' call reached him. How the man had gotten the number to his unlisted burner phone? He didn't know. Either way, he was finally in the town of Meyweather, attempting to track down Logan, who seemed the more talkative of the duo who'd sought him out roughly four months ago.

He knew tracking the man down would be hard—Shael daemons loved their freedom. What he did *not* expect was to end up at a cabin in the woods before a woman brimming with daemonic energy.

Against his chest, Crescent burned in the presence of such a twisted aura. The round pendant of silver was enchanted to sense suppressed daemonic power.

This woman wasn't even trying to hide hers. For the first time since he'd taken up this grim profession, he wanted to rip Crescent from his neck as it seared, burning hot.

This woman had to be a full-blooded daemon, though, at the moment, even that wasn't important. Why the hell did she have his brother's blade?

Lashing out, he grabbed her by the throat. "Where is he?" he demanded, nodding to the blade at her waist. "Don't play your games with me, daemon. I am not in the mood."

To his surprise, she maintained eye contact. This daemon was no stranger to combat—she'd been in this position before.

"Where is who?" Her voice was rough from pain, but Jace didn't feel a shred of guilt.

"You have his blade, daemon," he snarled, tightening his grip. "Where. Did. You. Get. It?"

She was frail for a daemon. What little was visible of her original skin color—amid the bruising on her face—paled even more. "Logan."

The soft whisper was the only sound she made before her jaw latched shut. From the defiance in her gaze, Jace suspected she wouldn't say anymore.

Which was perfectly fine with him. He had always liked doing things the hard way. Lunging forward, he shoved her into what seemed to be an empty cabin and closed the door behind him.

Her eyes widened with fear, and Jace cursed himself for the brief lack of foresight as she scrambled for his brother's blade. He didn't think the woman would attempt to use Krall against him, but her stupidity only allowed him to draw Jasper and show her firsthand how grave a mistake it was.

The daemonic knife hummed within his palm as he wrenched it from the sheath beneath his jacket and pressed the blade to her throat before she could even get Krall free. His other hand came to take the handle of his brother's blade.

And he swore. Invisible fire lanced up his arm, though there was no external sign of injury. *What the hell?* Shock made him wrench his hand away, giving the woman the opportunity to grab the weapon and wield it against him.

Okay. No more Mr. Nice.

One-handed, Jace let go of Jasper's hilt to flip the blade in the air and catch it again with the handle facing forward. Then, he jammed the butt of it into the woman's face. She crumpled with a low moan, dropping a black object that skidded past his feet.

Jace ignored whatever it was and moved to stand over her. She huddled with one hand pressed against her face, but those gray eyes blazed with only the smallest bit of fear.

Her resolve threw him off. Shouldn't she be spewing some evil manifesto, power, and chaos bullshit right about now? Swearing to call in the rest of her daemon minions to castrate him and string him up by his toes?

"Please," she managed to croak, surprising him even more. "I can give you money—whatever you want. Just leave."

Something in him balked at her tone—it wasn't like daemons to beg.

Still. She had Krall, Logan was nowhere in sight, and she looked like she'd taken a beating, lending to the theory that she'd somehow managed to overpower Logan and take his blade.

"Where is Logan?" he demanded outright. "Whether you speak or not, you'll still die—but tell me the truth, and I'll at least make your demise a little quicker."

She seemed to quake with terror, but Jace wasn't concerned—trapped in her human guise, the daemon had all but signed her own death warrant. A mortal body couldn't contain even a fraction of the daemon energy surging through her veins.

He'd be doing her a favor.

"Please," she whimpered.

Jace was almost fooled until he saw her hand creeping toward Krall. This time she was quicker, drawing the knife as he reached for her. Her fingers shook around the hilt as the blade jerked up, almost as if it had a mind of its own.

Pain lanced through his forearm, and he recoiled, alarmed as his blood dotted the floor. The little bitch had cut him —*deeply*.

No matter. Gritting his teeth, he delivered a kick to her chest, making her fall back with a whimper.

"You'll pay for that."

Again, she shocked him by shrugging off the pain and grasping for Krall, but Jace kicked the blade out of her reach. Pivoting, she lunged, half-crawling across the floor in her desperation to reach the door.

"Please, please, *please*," he heard her whimper as his hand cinched a long rope of bound black hair. Brutally, he wrenched her back, slamming her body into the side of a sturdy couch.

He must have used a little more force than he meant to, because she flipped over the surface entirely and landed on the other side with a thud.

Jace thumbed the sharp edge of his blade, prepared to finish the daemon off—after dragging Logan's whereabouts from her—when a sudden shout made him stop dead in his tracks.

"Serana!"

The sound drew his attention to the plastic object the woman had tossed aside—a cell phone. No doubt the little bitch had managed to make a call before he attacked her. She must have been this, Serana—not exactly a typical daemon name, but they were known to be creative.

Whatever. Whoever she'd called wouldn't be able to reach her in time anyway.

The woman seemed to realize this as he closed in on her, side-stepping the couch. Her eyes were wide—desperate—, and she tried in vain to scramble back, leaving a trail of blood over the floor.

"Serana! SERANA!"

At the caller's shouts, the woman almost seemed to shrink with dread. As she looked into his eyes, Jace could tell she had already realized her doom.

Had accepted it.

Even still, she released one last frantic moan that could have been a *name* beneath the pain.

One that sounded suspiciously like…

"I'll kill you!" The heated promise came from the cell, and at that exact moment, something in the familiar tone clicked in Jace's mind. "I'll kill you, you son of a bitch," the man on the other end of the cell phone growled, sounding more beast than human. "You touch her—and I will fucking *kill* you."

And Jace suddenly knew where his brother was, alright.

He glanced back at the woman, and only *now* could he recognize the distinctive scent of a daemonic half-breed mingling with the stench of human permeating the entire house.

Which meant only one thing...

Oops.

TWENTY-EIGHT

While her childhood hadn't involved much religious indoctrination, Serana did know one prayer. The same one ran through her mind as she stared at the man standing above her holding a knife.

God save my soul.

Kind of morbid, yeah. She could never quite understand why that particular prayer comforted her so much—according to most of the town, she didn't even have a soul.

Just like her father.

But…as she waited for death, she found herself whispering those words, wishing more than anything that God *could* save her soul. It was the only damn thing she had worth saving. Her one regret was calling Logan—why hadn't her fingers chosen to dial *anyone* but him?

"I'm sorry, Logan," she whispered, but by then, his growled threats had gone silent.

At the sound of his voice, however, her attacker froze. Without taking his eyes off her, he approached her cell in a fluid motion of dexterity and snatched it from the floor.

"Logan?" he grumbled into the speaker.

Fear lanced through Serana. "Don't hurt him." She sucked in a breath and began to crawl toward her would-be murderer. "Please, kill me—whatever you want—and leave. *Don't hurt him!*"

God, she couldn't bear anything happening to Logan because of her.

Oh, God. "Please," she begged the intruder, too horrified to look anywhere but the floor. "Kill me and leave, but don't hurt him. *Please—*"

"I'm not going to kill you."

Serana's head jerked up, her eyes wide. "Not killing" left all sorts of other scenarios that made her skin go cold.

The man didn't elaborate. He just eyed her cell phone in his hand as if it had insulted him.

"Logan?" he all but yelled into the receiver. When he didn't get a response, he tossed the thing aside and turned to her. Rather than murderous, his expression could be called wary. "Are you his lover?"

Serana flinched at the question. Even more so as the man sank down on one knee, his gaze boring into hers. "Logan?"

he asked, with what Serana got the feeling was deliberate slowness. "Are you his lover?"

Serana didn't know how to respond to that, so she didn't.

Her first thought had been that the man was some kind of wild mountain bandit, but besides a rather scruffy leather jacket, he looked relatively clean. The next leap in logic was that this was personal—one of her father's many victims aiming to take their revenge out on her.

But now…

"You're after Logan."

She was scanning the floor for Krall before the words even left her lips. Despite the pain racking through her body, she'd fight—do anything, to get this bastard to leave before getting to Logan.

Like what? a part of her countered. Unbidden, an image rose in her mind of Logan's chest with a blade sticking out of it. *Oh, God, no…*

"I don't want to hurt him." The sincerity in the man's tone was the only thing keeping her from crawling across the floor once she spotted her knife. *Logan's knife,* she mentally corrected. She could feel Krall's energy from here, aching to be wielded.

Still, she glanced back to find the man grimly appraising her. Whatever he saw, made the strong line of his jaw tighten even more.

"I didn't know he'd taken a lover," he murmured, almost to himself. "Especially not a mortal…"

Mortal? There wasn't time to ponder the odd word choice. The next moment, the man reached into his pocket and tossed something firm and round onto her lap.

"Use it," he urged. Serana watched, heart pounding, as he moved over to Krall but, to her surprise, he kicked the blade to her. "Did Logan leave you his knife?" he asked.

Serana nodded, but something kept her from picking up the knife. Her hand hovered, inches from the blade.

"What's wrong?" the man demanded, his eyes on her. "Is it damaged?"

"No. It—" She couldn't keep the truth in. "It wants me to…*hurt* you…"

Not just that—the energy blasting from Krall, like heat from a furnace, boasted ideas a lot more sinister. It wanted her to plunge it deep into the man's neck—his throat—twist, stab, pull, wrench. Feeding off her fear, the knife didn't just want to kill this man. It wanted to utterly destroy him.

Master! The voice was a whisper in her head, but no less threatening than the bellow from her dreams. *Wield me,* it pleaded in a lethal hiss. *Allow me to—*

"That salve will help with the pain." Serana flinched as the man's voice cut through Krall's grumbled threats. He watched her carefully, almost as if he sensed the lethal direction her thoughts had taken.

But he wasn't afraid, just curious.

Nervously, she let her hand fall to the floor, though she shifted closer to the blade. Then, she screwed off the top of the jar on her lap—anything for a distraction.

Just how much had Logan heard over the phone? What would he do? And what would happen to *her?*

The intruder's impassive stare didn't seem to hold an answer. "The salve will help," he insisted, and Serana couldn't tell if that was his shtick—have her treat her own wounds before going at her again?

Fingers shaking, she scooped out a glob of the paste-like substance onto her thumb and smeared it along the swelling she could feel rising over her right eye. The pain drumming through her body was so constant that she'd instinctively tuned it out—*an adrenaline rush*, a part of her explained. Only now, it chose to attack in full force, and she couldn't scoop up the yellowish paste fast enough.

The sudden relief made her moan out loud.

Despite everything—including the fact that he was a crazy knife-wielding murderer who would probably kill her— Serana found herself muttering thanks. The ointment helped. Though there wasn't a label around the black jar, she guessed it was a topical analgesic.

"I thought you were a daemon," he murmured after a moment, seeming to speak more to himself than to her.

Daemon? There wasn't time to process the strange word. The next moment, the man stiffened, head cocked to the side, as if catching wind of a far-away noise.

"Shit." He stowed his blade in the sheath at his side. "Tell him that I didn't know," he insisted, before stepping back, eyes on the door. "Tell him that I thought you were a daemon. That I didn't—"

An earth-shattering bang cut the man off. The next instant, the door seemed to fly off its hinges to crash into the wall—but even that wasn't as shocking as the figure who stood behind it.

Logan.

TWENTY-NINE

On second glance, this man couldn't be Logan. Blond hair, and emerald eyes were the only traits the lighthearted playboy she knew shared with the warrior in his place.

Rage didn't seem to describe the emotion surging through this stranger's veins. *Wrath* was more like it.

Serana shivered as those burning emerald eyes brushed over her once before moving to the intruder. In the second it had taken Logan to enter, the man had positioned himself by the fireplace. Far enough away that she wasn't in range when Logan lunged for him.

"You fucking bastard." It was the only thing he said, before striking the stranger in a spray of blood and the snap of what sounded like crunching bone.

Slam!

The whole floor trembled as the stranger went flying into the wall.

To be fair, he was no puny weakling.

He and Logan seemed to be equally matched, with the same muscular, broad-shouldered build. One thing going in Logan's favor, however, was that the stranger didn't fight back.

Not once. When Logan went for him again, he didn't lift so much as a finger in response to the fists that pummeled his jaw. His left eye. His chest.

The increasingly violent sounds of fists on flesh and muscle and bone made Serana shudder.

"Logan, stop—" Shakily, she lurched to her feet, fighting back a wave of dizziness. Her entire body throbbed, despite the soothing balm on her cheek. She had to lean against the couch just to find enough support to stand and suck in the air to call him again. "Logan!"

He didn't seem to hear her—or he didn't *want* to. Growling like an animal, he only delivered another punishing blow that sent the stranger collapsing to his knees.

The sound echoed like a gunshot, and this time Serana was pretty sure that he'd succeeded in breaking something vital.

"Logan…" She wanted to reach for him.

Wanted to run her fingers along his tanned jaw until it relaxed back into that casual line. Wanted to wrap her arms around those massive shoulders until he made some mocking joke about sex. She would have given anything to see lust fill those green eyes rather than this…

As he encircled the stranger's throat in a single fist, the man didn't even seem *human.*

"Logan," she whispered. "Please—"

"STOP!" The shout overpowered the violence, stilling even Logan's anger.

He froze, one bloody fist still clenched, and turned to the doorway where a massive stranger stood like a figure formed of shadow.

What is this, Serana couldn't help thinking as her vision started to blur, *the giant man convention?*

The newcomer's inky hair and dark eyes were way too familiar to belong to some shady mountain bandit, however.

"Let him go, Logan," Marcus said. His black eyes seemed to glow, and Serana flinched as he jerked his chin in her direction. "Go to Serana."

The sound of her name seemed to snap Logan from the darkness. He was beside her in an instant, slipping her in his arms before she even knew what was happening.

"Get her out of here," Marcus urged, before turning to the stranger with a frown. Did he know the man?

She didn't get the chance to ponder it. The next moment, Logan was carrying her in the direction of the bedroom as stiffly as a robot following commands.

"Salve…"

They both turned to find the wanna-be-bandit watching them, holding a hand against the side of his face, attempting to speak through a bloodied lip. Serana knew that she wouldn't be the only one sporting a massive black eye tomorrow. Judging from the way the guy flinched and clutched at his side, she suspected that he had a few busted ribs as well.

Strangely enough, he didn't seem angry to have been caught red-handed doing…whatever it was he was doing. Instead, he just looked…guilty.

"Use. It'll help." He gestured to the dark jar of salve with a nod.

Logan's eyes narrowed, and Serana figured that Marcus moving to block his path was the only thing that kept him from attacking the man all over again.

"You shut the fuck up," he said coldly.

Marcus casually walked between them to pick up the jar first. "Here—" He gave the bottle to Serana. "Logan, go. Help her…get cleaned up."

He gave her a grim appraisal with those dark eyes, and Serana didn't even want to guess how horrible she must have looked. Absolutely pathetic if Logan's grimace was anything to go by.

Finally, he carried her into a small bedroom and set her down on the bed. He handled her with nothing but gentleness—almost to a fault—but when he turned back to the door, he slammed it shut with so much aggression it shuddered on its frame.

Before she could so much as move, he was already in front of her, gingerly easing her sweater over her head. For once, he seemed purely focused on measuring the extent of her injuries, noting every scratch, scrape, and bruise.

"I'll kill him," he swore. "I'll fucking kill him."

"N-no you won't," Serana whispered, bracing a hand against his chest.

Obviously, the knife-wielding stranger was mentally disturbed, but it wasn't even pity for him that had her shuddering at the thought of Logan going back to finish what he started.

He was shaking. Literally trembling from head to toe. His heart pounded in an enraged rhythm that played beneath her palm.

"I'm alright," she insisted, flexing her fingers against the hardness of a smooth pec.

His concern confused her. Surprised her.

No one had ever…

"I'm alright."

He didn't look very convinced. Those dark eyes flashed with suspicion before he carefully pushed on her shoulder, urging her to lie back. He examined her entire body with detached clinical efficiency. Which was almost funny as she compared it with the way he'd "explored" her the night before.

Almost. At first, she made the mistake of thinking he inspected her so carefully purely out of curiosity—then she saw his eyes note every single injury. *Taking stock,* she realized. As if he planned to inflict every bruise on the man in the living room.

The thought terrified her, and she grabbed for the jar of salve.

"Help me with this," she managed to whisper.

Logan frowned as she pressed it into his hands, but she was gently insistent as she screwed off the top and used her own fingers to coax his into the thick paste. He didn't need much prodding after that—carefully, he started to smear the sticky substance on the rest of her bruised, swollen face, before moving down to her shoulder.

The task seemed to distract him from any murderous impulses—for now.

"What's this? I don't remember you having a tattoo here before."

Serana looked down as his thumb traced a spot just above her breastbone. It was slightly tender, most likely another bruise collected during her scuffle with the violent intruder. Only...

Its edges were far too sharp, more like a faint, indigo tattoo circular in shape, with concentric designs filling in the center.

"I don't know," she croaked, though Logan didn't seem alarmed. He silently applied more ointment to the spot and moved on, treating the rest of her aches and pains. Serana relented right until he reached for her pants and loosened the drawstring of her waistband. Her cheeks flamed as he eased the fabric down her legs and set it aside.

"Logan—"

"Shhh." There was nothing but concern in his gaze as it trailed down over her hip. Glancing down, Serana could see why—it was one giant, purpling bruise. She must have landed hard on her side when she fell…

Without a word, Logan applied salve to the worst of it and helped her redress.

"Stay here," he said, turning to the door. "When I come back, I'm taking you to the hospital."

Mentally, Serana rolled her eyes—*Would he ever get off that kick?*

"No." She tried to keep her tone soothing. She didn't bother lying about how she was "fine," despite a rapidly swelling right eye and blood dripping from a fresh cut on her forehead—and throat. Instead, she jumped right to the truth. "I don't want to go to the hospital."

Logan's eyes flashed. "Serana—"

"I *do* think we should call the police," she added in a rush.

Now, it was Logan's turn to look reluctant.

"We can't," he muttered.

"What? Why not?"

Serana gaped at him. He seemed to have had no trouble beating the man senseless, only to blanch when it came to calling the cops.

"Because…he's my *brother*."

She didn't even know how to begin to process that little tidbit of information, but he was already wrenching open the door before she could ask.

In the main room, Marcus stood over the stranger with crossed arms. When he saw Logan return, he offered a hand to the bloodied stranger and pulled him to his feet.

"Logan, listen—"

"What the hell, *Jacelyn*?" Logan snarled at the man, ignoring Marcus.

"It's *Jace*," the intruder corrected around a mouthful of blood, which he promptly spit onto the floor. Serana figured it was a wonder he could talk at all—she was sure one of Logan's blows had dislocated that firm jaw. "I thought I made that perfectly clear the first time?"

Logan growled, and it was only quick thinking from Marcus that kept him from going at Jace a second time. The bigger man shifted, intentionally blocking Logan's path.

"Just listen to what he has to say," he ordered in a tone that made Serana shiver. Logan just shrugged, eyes like poisoned gems as they glared into Jace's blue ones.

"So, start talking," he snarled, "you son of a—"

"Bitch?" Jace finished snidely. "You should know—she's *your* mother too."

"You motherfuck—"

"Logan!" This time Serana doubted that Marcus alone could keep Logan from launching himself at the man he called his brother.

"Start talking," he spat. "Though make it quick, so I can finish beating the living shit out of you—"

"I didn't know," Jace said quietly. From her position in the doorway, Serana could tell the sincerity in his tone was real. "Nobody told me that you'd taken a lover, let alone a *human.*"

"You didn't exactly stick around long enough to find out," Logan retorted—deliberately avoiding the whole "lover" aspect.

Why that made Serana's heart skip a beat, she had no idea.

"And you might want to brush up on your daemon hunting skills, *Jace,*" he added, curling his hands into fists. "Any idiot with fucking eyes could tell that she's human."

"You so sure about that?" Jace countered. Serana flinched as his eyes flickered over to her. "From where I'm standing, she doesn't seem so—that woman is practically on *fire* with daemonic energy."

Both Marcus and Logan whipped around to face her, and Serana could only stand there, wondering what the hell the man meant by…daemonic energy.

"What the hell did you do to her, huh? Think of me as the villain all you want, but if I had killed her, it would only have been putting her out of her misery. If she isn't a daemon, she can't possibly withstand the amount of energy—"

"Shut up," Logan croaked, but his eyes were wide with something that Serana recognized as…fear.

That makes two of us, she thought helplessly. *Daemon? Human?*

She could barely follow the strange conversation, and something in Logan's tone—and the fact that he'd used the same odd phrasing—left a bad taste in her mouth.

Who the hell were these people?

"Logan." Marcus' voice was intentionally soft as he moved forward to place a hand on the man's shoulder. "Take her out of here."

"No!" Serana didn't even realize she'd spoken until all three men turned to gape at her, as if she'd grown three heads.

Logan looked the most shaken of all. Those green eyes never left her face.

"I'm not leaving," she insisted, feeling the need to cross her arms over her chest. "What the hell is going on?"

She didn't know where to start.

Maybe with why they hadn't called the police on this mysterious Jace? Or at least an ambulance, due to the way he flinched as he shifted his weight on the balls of his feet?

Or why Logan looked so utterly terrified?

Or how in the hell Marcus was always so damn calm?

She opened her mouth, intending to demand one of those many answers…when the world shifted underneath her feet. She found herself falling sideways, almost in slow motion, as everything seemed to turn on its head.

"Serana!" She wasn't quite sure if she actually heard Logan shout her name, or just guessed from the way his mouth stretched as he lunged forward like a video stuck on pause.

It was only when an alarming ringing sound began to toll in her ears that she realized she was fainting. The thought was almost funny—she wasn't the kind of woman who did shit like swoon.

But as the pain faded, she realized that all those dramatic bimbos in old movies must have had the right idea.

After a morning like the one she'd had, trying to be strong was overrated.

So, as her vision turned black, she gave in to the darkness.

Why the hell not?

Poor Serana had no idea that—while she slept in the bedroom—her cabin was now the stage of a makeshift family reunion starring him, Marcus, and their daemon-hunting asshole of a brother. Logan made a mental note to make it up to her later, right after he finished beating Jacelyn into a bloody pulp.

His only concern was that he didn't know whether to include Marcus on his unofficial hit list. The bastard had called the hunter here after all. To his credit, their elder brother seemed more intent on peace than taking a side in their burgeoning rivalry for the time being.

"Now that you're caught up," Marcus said, having just finished reciting everything from the issue of Krall and Serana to Logan's stint in prison. "What do you think? Have you heard of them, these Protectors of the Dawn?"

He addressed Jace, who leaned against the wall near the fireplace, nursing a swelling jaw with a bag of ice taken from the freezer.

"No," the hunter replied, his voice slightly garbled. "But I know enough to suspect they aren't daemon hunters or even a cult dedicated to preventing the apocalypse. They most likely work for Liva, and you just led them right to the harbinger."

"Liva keeps tabs on all of us," Logan pointed out, feeling a need to defend himself. If anyone was going to judge his actions, it wouldn't be a psychopath who'd nearly beaten an unarmed woman to death. Aware of the danger Serana was in, he stood near the door to the bedroom, hoping that she was okay while simultaneously praying that she slept through this entire discussion. "I'm sure our dear old mother has known where Mirabelle was all along."

"But *we* haven't," Jace countered. "Don't tell me you haven't suspected as much—she's drawn us to the harbinger for a reason. Have you stopped to think why that might be? The good thing is that you've foiled her plan by attacking that mortal. I think you have a very clear choice to make. You kill the mortal woman, reclaim Krall, and then we all get as far from here as possible."

Logan lurched forward, but Marcus held up a hand to stop him in his tracks. Addressing Jace, the Raeth spoke for them both. "No."

"I wasn't asking," Jace snarled, lowering his bag of ice. The darkening bruises on his face highlighted his angular facial features that neither Marcus nor Logan shared. "*You* made this my business. If that mortal foiled whatever plan Liva had in store, then I have a vested interest in ensuring that plan is never carried out. By any means necessary. I suggest you don't get in my way."

"I dare you to touch her." Logan balled his hands into fists. "She's been fucked up enough."

"What do you mean?" Marcus interjected.

Logan eyed him warily before confessing the small things he'd noticed but had yet to truly ponder. "I saw a mark on Serana's chest that wasn't there before. Remember what that witch said? She has enough on her plate, so if you so much as look at her wrong, you daemon-hunting son of a witch, I will kill you—"

"Or," Marcus quietly interjected, "we can put that aside for now and focus on the more pressing threat. Donovan has a 'device' rumored to predict the future. I think we need to discover exactly what it may be *while* we search for answers about what might be happening to Serana."

"You prefer chasing a fortune-teller over helping Logan regain control of his blade?" Jace demanded.

"No," Marcus said without a hint of guilt. Bathed in shadow, it was evident that, of the three men, he was the biggest, capable of taking on even a daemon hunter should the urge strike him. "I prefer to prioritize what we focus on. For the moment, Serana is safe with Logan, and that's where she will stay. Solving the issue of Krall can come later—"

"And making sure she doesn't die," Logan felt the need to add, glaring at Jace. "By any means."

Marcus nodded. "But a daemon lord with a fortune-telling device? It sounds a bit too farfetched. A man like Donovan wouldn't hoard some useless trinket. I believe its real identity may be far more nefarious."

Jace stroked his chin, ignoring the blood drying there. "You think it could be another child from the prophecy?"

Marcus nodded. "Donovan is a powerful Klaen. That race is rumored to have once possessed the power of foresight."

"That's a fairy tale," Logan said, crossing his arms. "Some say Shaels can fly. I can tell you personally that's bullshit."

"Bullshit, maybe," Marcus said. "But for a long time, I've suspected that at least some of us could still be in the daemon realm. I have yet to find all of Liva's children. It would make sense for one to be a Klaen."

"Another brother?" Logan asked, attempting to picture this potential sibling. If they were part Klaen and related to a lord as powerful as Donovan, then he was about as excited to meet them as he'd been meeting Mirabelle.

Marcus shrugged. "Either way, we need to know for sure."

"You want to steal from a daemon lord?" Jace's voice was deadly quiet.

"I want to stay one step ahead of our mother," Marcus clarified. "The question is, are you in or out?"

With Serana's life on the line, Logan didn't even hesitate. "Yes. Count me in."

Jace, however, sighed. "I'll do what I can to keep you both out of prison, but it's a foolish plan."

"But it's a start," Marcus countered.

He had a point. It wasn't an ideal event for their first sibling outing, but what better bonding experience than pissing off a daemon lord in the hopes of adding to their mismatched family?

And to keep Serana safe, a task that Logan suddenly felt determined to undertake.

Despite any brother who dared to get in his way.

~ Logan and Serana's story continues in Daemon's Bane ~

A Word from the Author

Hey there!

Thank you so much for reading! If you enjoyed the story, please leave a review and recommend the book to any friend you think would love this twisted world. You'd have my eternal gratitude. Even a short sentence goes a long way!

Then, come join the rest of us dark romance lovers in my Facebook Group where you can get snippets, sneak peeks of upcoming books and even help vote on aspects of future novels.

Come to the dark side:
https://www.facebook.com/groups/lanasbeautifulmonsters/

WANT MORE STUFF TO READ?
Join my newsletter and get a **free book**! Plus, you get to stay updated with any new releases, random giveaways and exclusive sneak peeks!
https://www.lanaskybooks.com/newsletter

Other Novels: https://lanaskybooks.com/

FREE BOOK - JOIN MY NEWSLETTER

DARK, TWISTED ROMANCE

Join my newsletter and get a **free book**! Plus, you get to stay updated with any new releases, random giveaways and exclusive sneak peeks!

https://www.lanaskybooks.com/newsletter

ABOUT THE AUTHOR

Lana Sky is a reclusive writer in the United States who spends most of her time daydreaming about complex male characters and parenting her Cockapoo Joey. She writes dark, twisted romance across several genres. Her titles include everything from mafia romance to vampires.

facebook.com/AuthorLanaSky

twitter.com/lanasky101

amazon.com/author/lanasky

pinterest.com/lanasky101

goodreads.com/lanasky

instagram.com/lanasky101

bookbub.com/authors/lana-sky

tiktok.com/@author_lana_sky

ALSO BY LANA SKY

For more titles by Lana Sky, please visit:

https://www.lanaskybooks.com